The River Village

Wali Shaaker

ISBN-13: 978-1505324914
ISBN-10: 1505324912

To Roya, Wasim, and Palatin

ONE

Kabul, winter 1980 - Mother's cry pierced through the wall separating Masih's room from that of his parents. Shaken awake, he sat on his bed and rubbed his eyelids. He listened for a few seconds. Mother wasn't the only one shouting in distress. Father too sounded frustrated. The thirteen-year-old had heard his parents argue before, but they had never yelled at each other with such intensity. No, it wasn't a nightmare. He tried, but couldn't understand what they were arguing about as their voices sounded muffled through the concrete barrier.

Then, he heard a third voice—a stranger's voice that sounded calm, as if he was explaining a process or making an argument. Who was this man? At hours past midnight, no one, not even a friend of Father should have been allowed in the house, let alone inside their bedroom. Was he a burglar? Was he going to hurt them? Something must be terribly wrong. His heart began to race, as he noticed a sliver of light penetrating through the crack of the closed door of his room.

Terrified and confused, Masih yanked the blanket away, jumped out of his bed, and barefoot dashed through the ice-cold cement hallway.

Father was stepping out of the bedroom, wearing a navy blue jacket over his traditional white clothes. As he gritted his teeth, veins popped on his temples and his eyes widened in fear. The tips of his disheveled hair hung over his wire-framed glasses. Masih's heart dropped when he saw two soldiers gripping his trembling arms on each side. However, he did not seem to resist the arrest. He had tried to explain to the intelligence officer and the military men accompanying him that he had no connections with the antigovernment forces, the *mujahedin* at all. And the fact that some twenty years ago he was educated in the U.S. did not necessarily mean that he was a spy of the CIA. But they didn't believe him. Prior to planning the raid on the doctor's house, they had received reports that he had been trying to undermine the Marxist regime by spreading antirevolutionary, pro-imperialist propaganda.

Looking inside his parents' bedroom, Masih saw books and papers scattered all over the floor. The intruders had searched every bookshelf, every box, and every closet. Yet, they had found no evidence indicating that Sharif was a CIA agent. They had also paid a visit to Masih's bedroom, only to realize that there was nothing there worthy of investigation. Besides, if the boy woke up, he would likely begin to make a scene, crying and clinging on to his father. Separating the two would be an unnecessary waste of time and a disturbance for the entire operation. It was best not to wake him up.

On several occasions, Father himself had told Masih that he was supposed to be a *ba-ghairat*, an honorable Afghan boy, and that he must never be afraid of anything. But behind the clear lenses of his spectacles, his eyes seemed glossy with a layer of profound grief and intense fear. For the first time, Masih had witnessed his father not merely scared, but terrified. He could not detect the slightest trace of hope anywhere on his face—a kind face, which appeared as white as the color of the robe he wore at work every day. Yet, Father managed to maintain a defiant expression, keeping his chin militantly up.

At five foot ten, Dr. Sharif was not a small man. But a much taller, burly *Khadist*, a secret service agent in a black suit and a wrinkled red tie towered over him from behind. Tips of a dark mustache hung loosely on two sides of his wide mouth. As Masih ran toward Father, Dr. Sharif freed his arms with a powerful yank that stunned his young captors. He pressed his son's head against his chest and kissed it, drawing the scent of his straight hair into his lungs. Then, cupping his hands around Masih's face, he wrinkled his forehead, assuming a serious expression, bent down to meet his eyes, and cleared his throat, "Take care of your mother. Always obey her, and finish school."

He laid a kiss on each cheek of the face that always reminded him of his own boyhood, and then let go of him.

"Father, what's going on? Where are they taking you? Are you coming back tomorrow?" Masih asked, fear striking his young heart. He knew of two boys in school whose fathers had been imprisoned in Pul-e Charkhi, Afghanistan's most dreaded jailhouse, and of one other boy, whose older brother was kidnapped on his way home from Kabul University by men in military uniform. No one had ever heard from them again.

"*Bachem,* Son, I'll be okay."

The pleading voice of Mother quivered from behind the broad shoulders of the mustached man in black, "I beg you. Fear God. Don't take him, *please*! He has done nothing wrong."

Judging by the coarse sound of her voice and the look in her bloodshot eyes, Masih could tell that for a long while his mother had been weeping and pleading for the release of her husband.

Then, he caught a glimpse of a handgun dangling on the *Khadist,* secret police officer's right hip. The soldier who clutched Father's right arm had a machinegun slung over his shoulder, and the one grabbing his left arm had secured a firm grip around the midsection of an identical weapon. Masih could do nothing to rescue Father. And no, he was not going to implore for his release either. These men had already decided to take him away. Besides, begging for mercy would not have been honorable; it was not what Father would have approved. He circled his arms around Father's waistline, as though trying to restrain him from leaving.

"Father, I will wait for you," his tears left dark marks on Sharif's clothes.

"It's okay son, *Khoda mehraban ast*, God is kind," he forced those words through a chocked throat, and patted Masih's back.

Then, he turned and hugged his wife, Nadia, the only woman he had ever loved.

"There must have been a misunderstanding. I will be back in no time," he assured her with a trembling voice. Through a brief eye contact, lasting only a couple of seconds, they affirmed their love for each other without uttering a word.

"Don't worry *hamshira*, sister. As I said, tomorrow as soon as the investigation is over, I will personally bring Dr. Sharif home. I promise," the intelligence officer said to Nadia, trying to sound sincere.

Yet, both Nadia and the Khadist knew that the assurance meant nothing. He said those words and allowed the farewell to proceed only to keep Dr. Sharif's wife and son calm. He had executed similar night raids at least a dozen times before. Usually, if the wife and the children of the detainee begin to wail and scream, begging for mercy, the neighbors would wake up, and the mission would turn into a show. Under such circumstances, it would become too embarrassing to get the suspect into the vehicle while everyone watched, standing on the doorsteps or the flat rooftops of their houses.

In addition, the officer didn't want to stay there any longer than necessary. He just wanted to finish the mission and go home—to his own wife and children.

Father sat in the rear seat of an idling *Rosee*, a Soviet jeep, and the soldiers sat next to him on each side. Sharif looked out of the half-fogged window to his right. He watched his wife and son standing on the sidewalk and staring at the vehicle with tearful eyes.

Nadia and Masih's hearts sank as the doors of the vehicle slammed shut.

***

The burly man occupied the seat next to the driver who took the vehicle along with Father, and disappeared into the gloom of the night.

TWO

Kabul, winter 1979 – Masih tried to ignore the irritating noise of the military aircraft that buzzed over the city. About every hour, one of the stout transporters headed either north or south. During the past several weaks the aircrafts, loaded with heavy military equipment and personnel have been flying back and forth between Moscow and Bagram Airbase.

"Why are there so many airplanes in the sky?" Masih asked as he held the spool to help his father fly the kite.

"They are coming from *Shorawi*, the Soviet Union," Dr. Sharif answered, keeping his eyes fixed on the giant kite. As the wind billowed under its belly, it yanked on the glass-coated thread and caused the spool to spin violently in between Masih's fingers.

"Go on. Watch what they are doing, and watch carefully," Father whispered as if the kite could hear him. Although Dr. Sharif knew that it was impossible for his kite to reach the aircraft, slash its chest, and send it tumbling to the ground, he fantasized about it anyway.

***

That night, when a thin sheath of ice had covered the outer surface of the windows, a fierce shuddering of Masih's bed and the rattling of the house's walls shook him awake. Startled, he asked himself, *"What is happening? An earthquake?"* Unable to see much in the dark, he wrapped himself in his blanket.

The commotion woke up Dr. Sharif and Nadia as well. Minutes later, the convoy arrived behind the doctor's house, pushing up toward the Bagh-e Bala hills. As the military vehicles roared forward, their chains chewed up the road and shook the ground underneath.

Dr. Sharif slowly opened the front gate a crack and peered through. What he saw amazed and at the same time horrified him. A flood of headlights, seeming to stretch all the way from Bagram Airbase, steadily crept toward Paghman Valley.

In the midst of the darkness and a heavy fog of dust and smoke, he witnessed what he had only read of in the history books occurring over and again in Afghanistan—foreign invasion.

"Go back to bed. The Soviets are passing by. It's going to be alright," he said to Masih, who stood behind him, shivering in the freezing temperature.

Is it really going to be okay? Sharif asked himself, and dreaded that this might be only a wishful thought.

Sharif pulled the comforter over his son and blew out the candle that Masih had lit just minutes ago, *"Sher-e Padar,* Dad's lion, don't ever be afraid of anything, okay?"

"I am not scared. I am just mad." He shut his eyes.

***

When Masih woke up, it was too quiet to be morning. The sun had risen, but the traffic noise, which could normally be heard from the street, was silenced. The Soviet tanks were still out there, engines killed. He could see some of their antennas extending beyond the wall that separated the front yard from the sidewalk. The fume of diesel still polluted the air. As he cracked open the gate, he saw the most monstrous vehicles that he had ever seen in his life. A Soviet tank seemed even larger than the elephant in the Zoo. No wonder the entire house was shaking last night.

He stepped on the sidewalk, and looked to his left and right, unable to locate the head or the tail of the convoy. The serpent stretched beyond his field of view on both sides.

"Let's go son, find out what this is all about," Father said, standing behind him. His *Mazari* cloak, as thick as a comforter with red, blue, and green stripes, draped over his shoulders. Masih zipped his leather jacket and began to walk next to his father. They hiked uphill toward Bagh-e Bala, stepping on scattered patches of snow and ice on the sidewalk.

Wearing thick woolen uniforms and furry round military hats, the Soviet invaders sat on top of their vehicles and enjoyed the crisp air under Kabul's sunny winter sky. Some lit up cigarettes; others scooped food, most likely *haram*, forbidden in Islam pork out of a can and ate it without minding the taste. Many yet remained almost motionless, glancing around and trying not to appear nervous. Perhaps they were as shocked to see crowds of mainly Afghan boys and men for the first time as were the Afghans by their sudden visit.

"Zdrast, kahk dyeh lah?" said a street vendor in Russian, hoping to make a sale. The Soviets answered with a nod, a fake smile, and a few words of their own, which including the vendor, nobody seemed to understand.

Masih realized that he had been mistaken in assuming that the tanks were the most frightening machines. The roar of two helicopters hovering above made the hair stand on his skin. The belly of one almost brushed against the tip of an acacia tree. Accompanied by a tornado of crisp air, the flying monsters circled around the neighborhood not too far above the convoy. Exhibiting heavy weapons mounted on their sides, they flew at low altitude to intimidate the crowd with their sheer size and deafening roar. Masih was certain that if they opened fire, no one standing on those sidewalks would return home alive. Yet, no one seemed to care.

***

As they were walking, a soldier with facial features similar to the Uzbek carpet merchants of downtown Kabul locked eyes with Masih. He seemed relaxed, sitting atop his armored vehicle. The young man, who appeared no more than four years older than Masih, smiled and shouted, *"Salam alaikum*, peace be upon you."

For a moment or two, Masih kept his gaze locked with the soldier's and then spit far enough to hit the chain of the tank on which he was sitting.

"Wa alaikum assalam, peace be upon you too," Dr. Sharif shot back and kept walking.

Some fifty steps farther, he stopped and faced Masih, "Listen. You are a Muslim, an Afghan. Every time someone greets you with *Salam*, even if he is your enemy, you answer with *Wa-alaikum assalam*, not with spitting. What you did was not right. Do you understand?"

"*Bale*, yes, "Masih mumbled, focussing on the frozen sidewalk."
"Look at me. I didn't hear you," Father stepped forward to face him.
Lifting his chin, Masih answered, "*Bale Padar jan*, yes Father," then he
added, "I don't like them. They have no right to be here."

"Me neither. But don't worry, son. They won't last too long in
this country. Nobody has."

The sight of the Soviet soldiers reminded Masih of the stories
Father had told him about the British invasion of Afghanistan. He
couldn't remember the details of all the events and the names of the
people who led the freedom movement. But he knew that only a few
decades ago, the Afghans had been able to fight off the British and
defeat them on three occasions. Every time Masih heard those
stories, he felt the hair standing on the back of his neck. He admired
his ancestors, those honorable men and women who did not bow to
the British bullies and made the ultimate sacrifice. Would he ever be
able to exhibit such bravery? The question twirled in his mind.

But in this day and age, meeting the Soviets on the battlefield
would be an entire new challenge. When the Brits invaded,
helicopters and tanks didn't exist. Besides, according to Father,
Afghans possessed better guns than the enemy did. This time,
however, it is much more difficult, if not impossible to get rid of the
foreigners. Where would the *mujahedin*, freedom fighters get the
firepower that matched that of the Soviets? Despite the disparities in
fire power and technology, it would be an honor to fight against the
Soviets. But, would his parents allow him to become a *mujahed*, a
fighter? As these thoughts rushed through his head, his heart
pounded with excitement.

Unlike most other pedestrians, who stared at the convoy with
curiosity and confusion, Dr. Sharif kept his gaze fixed on a point far
away. As they walked, he too was thinking about the future of his son
and his wife, and the future of Afghanistan. Despite his assuring
remarks to Masih, he feared that the advent of a bleak period was
inevitable, much darker than he ever could have imagined.

THREE

On the last day of winter and the final day of the Afghan calendar year, Masih and Nadia woke up at five in the morning as the sun was still crawling up on the other side of the mountains. An hour later, they left their house in Kart-e Parwan and headed for *Deh Darya*, The River Village about forty miles to the northwest of Kabul. To reach the village, they boarded one bus to Maiwand Boulevard in downtown, and took another toward Deh Darya. The second bus was owned and operated by *Khalifa*, the master, Zaman, a longtime family friend.

Dents and scratches on every side marked the insipid white paint of the battered vehicle. As she began to roar and roll, her windows shivered and metal collided against metal, plastic, or glass. With each gear that Khalifa Zaman shifted, her aged diesel engine growled louder, like a wounded beast.

Driving on the dirt road outside the city's parameters, Khalifa constantly turned and twisted the steering wheel, less than an inch away from his protruding stomach. He avoided potholes, rocks, and puddles, mushrooming one after the other on the way to the village. Despite the fact that he had traveled along this road back and forth six days a week for many years, from time to time he would miss an obstacle. One of the tires would fall into a pothole or roll over a rock. The *"palang,"* tiger, as Khalifa Zaman called it, would bounce up and down and swing from side to side; a kayak caught in a turbulent ocean. The passengers, sitting or standing, would then have to hold on to any piece of metal or plastic they could reach to avoid banging heads with each other or against the ceiling.

Nadia and her son were used to the ride and its hills and valleys. While Masih had made dozens of journeys to Deh Darya in this vehicle, Nadia has been riding in it since the time she was a student at Kabul University's School of Literature. Back then, Masih wasn't even born. Khalifa had struck a friendship with Nadia and her husband. In fact, over the years, he had made friends with most of his regular passengers, including Deh Darya's residents. Therefore, now and then, villagers would invite him and his family to participate in special events and attend parties.

***

Deh Darya settled near a riverbank and on the foothills of the Hindu Kush. From those mountains, streams of melted snow poured into the river passing through the village wineries, orchards, vegetable gardens, and lush fields of wheat and maize. It gave life to the village and its surroundings.

On the side of the road that led to the village, Sori's mother, Mahro laid to rest in the cemetery. Nadia and Masih paused in front of her grave, prayed, and continued to stride toward the first mud house on the outskirt of Deh Darya, where Mahro once lived with her husband, Sekandar, and their sons, Jawad and Aziz. On the opposite side, the unruly river galloped down the mountains, crashing against rocks and boulders of different sizes and shapes.

Apple, cherry, pear, and peach trees stood naked in Baba Sekandar's orchard and vegetable garden. Attached to it was the house that he had built with his own hands and with help from the chief, Qayoum Khan, the man who owned most of the land in the area.

Nadia and Masih crossed the road and continued to walk under the aged mulberry and *kingberry*, blackberry trees—all lined up along the riverbank. Judging by the thickness and rugged look of their wrinkled trunks, someone must have planted them a long time ago— someone considerate, who had placed them in equal distances. The ample space allowed them to spread their roots, stretch their arms, and fill them with as many leaves and berries as they wished. No one knew whose ancestor had done such a great service to the community. Nevertheless, many believed that this person must have been one of the first individuals who had settled near the river, hence laying the foundation for Deh Darya.

As they arrived at Baba Sekandar's house, Masih picked up the heavy knocker and tapped it against the thick metal plate attached to the gate. A few seconds later, he heard the jingle of Sori's bangles on the other side of the nine feet mud-wall as she approached to open the gate.

"Who is it?" Sori asked.

Nadia answered, "It is your aunt."

Sori unhooked the chain in a hurry and opened the gate, "*Salam*, hello, what a surprise!" her eyes glittering with excitement.

Trying to conceal at least some of his own delight, Masih mumbled a simple greeting, "*Salam.*"

The women hugged and planted several kisses on each other's cheeks. Next, it was Masih's turn. As usual, Sori bent a notch and clenched his face with her scrawny right hand, burying her thumb in one cheek, and four fingers in the other. She then deposited two loud and juicy kisses on each side of his face, the kind to which people of Deh Darya referred as *pachchi*, with sound effect and all. At first, Masih's face changed color to a bright pink. But by the time he had stepped inside, it blazed with red, not only because he was embarrassed, but also because he was irritated.

When was she going to treat him like an adult? When was *anybody* going to treat him like a man? After all, in less than three months, Masih would turn fifteen. Still he had to get permission from his mother for everything he did, and be treated like a little boy by Sori, who by the way, was only four years older than he was. So what if he had not begun to shave yet? So what if he was an inch or two shorter than she was? One of these days, he would strike back: *Don't treat me like a kid. I am FIFTEEN years old!*

Regretfully, once again he had lost that opportunity.

Nadia, Masih, and their cheerful host crossed the front yard. They passed by Sori's rose garden. Preparing to thaw, about a dozen frozen bushels huddled in the center of the yard. In about four to six weeks, red, yellow, pink, and white buds would begin to bloom, surrounded by burgeoning baby leaves. Then, the front yard would turn into a blossoming mini garden.

The guestroom was better exposed to the sunshine, always tidy, and a couple of feet wider than the other room across the small hallway.

"Sori *Jan*, my soul," Nadia always called to her with this expression of endearment—the way Sori's mother would have called her, "come my daughter, sit next to me," she said, leaning against a spotless white pillow.

From a china teapot, Sori poured green tea sprinkled with a pinch of cardamom powder into aunt Nadia's cup, "I just brewed some tea, as if I knew you were coming. Let me prepare for lunch; I'll be right back." She stepped out and disappeared into the kitchen across the yard.

Sitting on one of the two mattresses in the room, Nadia turned to Sekandar and asked one of the usual icebreakers, "So, how has the weather been Baba?"

"*Wallah*, by God, not too bad. With His blessing, we have had many solid weeks of snow and rainfall. *Ensha'Allah*, God-willing we won't be left hungry." He took a long sigh and added, "Only if those Godless government boys leave us alone." Old age had carved deep creases around the bags hanging under his green eyes, and across his wide forehead. Not even a strand of dark hair had tainted his thick, well-kept beard.

"That's surprising. You are not even a feudal like Qayoum Khan."

"The problem is not that they want to bother me. Actually, they want to help me," Baba chuckled, exposing a handful of unhealthy teeth left intact in his mouth.

"How so?"

"Well, based on government's number-eight *Farman*, decree, they are distributing most of Qayoum Khan's land to landless farmers like me. They are taking it from the king and giving it to the beggar, so to speak," he sighed, reaching for the hot teacup and holding it on the palm of his craggy wrinkled hand, as if he didn't even feel the high temperature.

"Did they actually come and tell you that?"

"Last month they came in the mosque. Mulla Salim didn't seem happy about it, but they came in anyway. They announced that they'll begin distributing most of Qayoum Khan's land to landless farmers before the beginning of the new growing season."

"What are you going to do now?" Nadia asked, frowning.

"There is nothing I can do. Of course, I want to tell them what they are doing is against God's rule. Too bad, they are communists. They follow the Lenin's Law. The land belongs to the person who works it. That's what they say; that's what they believe. But that's not what *we* believe. We are Muslims, you know. We say the land belongs to whoever is blessed and destined by God to own it. Trouble is, as soon as you mention God, they think you are the enemy."

"Yes Baba, I have seen their slogans all over the city. But you have always stood behind Qayoum Khan, in his good days and in his bad. You are a man of honor."

"You know what? Even if it were *halal*, permissible in Islam, I would never agree to loot Qayoum Khan's land. My conscience and my *ghairat*, honor wouldn't allow it."

"They don't know anything about our ways, Baba. They think what they are doing is helping the poor, making people happy. But in reality, they are making everybody's lives miserable," Nadia said, shaking her head.

"The good news is that Sarwar has just come back from Pakistan. He is putting together a group of *mujahedin*, fighters. My sons are the first to sign up. This time, if those apostates return, I am sure we can deal with them," Baba leaned against the wall with a fixed gaze at the wooden beams running under the ceiling.

Helpless in offering an alternate solution, Nadia said, "God is merciful. He will show us some light."

***

In a small windowless kitchen near the well, Sori lifted her head up from the blazing mouth of the *tanor*, clay-oven. Then, she stretched another dough ball on the smooth surface of a long wooden board. It was soon to be transformed into a steaming bread loaf. The aroma of smoke mixed with the delicious waft of freshly baked bread filled the air.

"I think you are in trouble. Tomorrow is *Nawroz*, New Year's Day," Sori said.

"What do you mean?" Masih asked. He squatted with his back leaning against the blackened wall.

"Well, Baba is going to take you to the mosque, and you don't even know how to pray. Aren't you worried about that?"

"I know how to pray," he answered swiftly.

"Really? And when did you learn to do that?"

"Father taught me. I have prayed in the mosque with him many times. Last Eid, I prayed with Baba too."

"Yes, but that Eid was months ago. By now, you must have forgotten how to pray," she said trying not to grin.

"No, I remember. I pray all the time. I am not a *kafer*, an infidel like you."

"My God! Shame on you calling me *kafer*. You are the *maktabi*, school boy, not me," she smiled.

"What are you talking about? You have been going to school for the past twenty years."

"You are insulting me now. I have never been a lazy student," Sori laughed.

"We'll see. You might be right only if you graduate."

"For your information, there won't be any graduation for me. I used to be a student and a good one too, but no more," Sori said. Then she leaned down, reached inside the oven, and whacked the elongated dough at the smoldering wall licked by the flame from the bottom.

"Why not?"

"Well, last week, that *Chaqo-kash*, knife-fighter who calls himself a *mujahed*, burned the school down."

She was referring to none other than Sarwar, Qayoum Khan's only son. He had earned the nickname by carrying a knife in his pocket and not hesitating to use it in a fight.

"What? Why would he do something like that?" Masih shook his head in disbelief.

"Apparently, during a Friday prayer, Mulla Salim had issued a *fatwa*, decree that those who send their kids to school are committing a sin. He said the government was brainwashing the children to turn them into communists. He gave people a choice: stop sending your kids to school, or it will be scorched."

"And people didn't listen?"

"Most didn't. I didn't. Education is my God-given right. Plus, I thought he was just bluffing. I didn't think that anybody, especially a mulla could actually destroy a school. I don't know, maybe that is how God wants things to be. First, He took my mother away, and now He sent Sarwar to ruin all of my dreams." She wiped her cheeks with the corner of her colorful scarf and bent toward the fire to take out a baked bread. Clearly, it wasn't just the sting of smoke rising from the oven that flooded Sori's eyes with tears.

Was there anything Masih could tell her to alleviate the sadness of a lost dream, the pain of watching a bright future fade away?

"God is merciful," he said the same reassuring phrase that he had heard from adults all his life, "once the Soviets are gone, everything will be okay."

As tears rolled down Sori's cheek, she managed to force a smile, "You sound just like your father."

Although Masih had no idea how the Afghans could make the Soviet tanks and helicopters disappear, he meant what he said. Battling a superpower was not going to be easy. Yet, if they defeated the Brits, not once but three times, they could beat the Soviets too?

***

On every occasion that Sori went to Kabul, or Dr. Sharif visited Deh Darya, they talked about the health clinic that, one day, together they would establish in the village. She would ask Uncle Doctor a number of questions about becoming a doctor, discuss scientific matters, and seek advice on how to pass the entrance exam for Kabul University. Dr. Sharif would patiently listen to her concerns and answer her questions. Then, they would somehow engage in a debate about an issue concerning women's rights, health, or education. Dr. Sharif had attended a medical school in the U.S. Therefore, he would offer his comparative analysis of women's struggles and achievements in America versus those of their counterparts in Afghanistan. Sori, of course, would express her own opinions, many of which did not match those of Dr. Sharif's.

He insisted that the plight of Afghan women would improve if the economy developed and if the political system, by some miracle, transformed into a democratic one. Often, he would offer the example of democracy in action in the U.S. as he had witnessed it firsthand. "Look at America," he would say, extending his arm toward the window, as if America was outside in the courtyard, "as democracy took roots there, women and minorities were able to secure their rights. If a democratic system were established in Afghanistan, the same could happen here."

"Uncle, Afghanistan is not America," she would argue, "Afghan women can't afford to wait a hundred years for democracy to happen. If the conditions are not right, they have to change it, *make* it right."

As minutes passed by and the debate boiled on, Sori spoke louder and less clear, using frequent head and hand gestures. Almost every time though, when she returned to Deh Darya, or he went back to Kabul, Sori wondered if she had crossed the line with excessive audacity. Her father's criticism of her bold, outspoken style with Dr. Sharif didn't help either. Remorse would burden her mind until she saw Uncle Doctor again, and took the opportunity to apologize for what could have been perceived as rude behavior.

***

"Sori, you shouldn't apologize for expressing your views. You know what they say; nobody distributes candy in a fight. Always voice your opinions." Not once did Dr. Sharif think that she was ill mannered. In fact, he admired Sori's ability and courage to articulate and express her thoughts with such great passion. However, despite their disagreements, what they always agreed on was the necessity for establishing a health clinic in Deh Darya. Repeatedly, they thought out and talked about how to build and manage this clinic. Once it is established, no other woman would lose her life during childbirth, the way Sori's mother did. Deh Darya and the surrounding villages needed a health facility where mothers could get their children vaccinated, and where the elderly could seek treatment for their ailments.

***

With a health clinic in the area, villagers would no longer have to travel long distances to reach a doctor in Kabul. This clinic would be a place within people's reach, a place they could rely on to obtain health services.

Sori had dared to dream and had the confidence to believe in herself. Therefore, she had won Dr. Sharif's admiration and support. "God willing, we will build it together. I am as committed to this project as you are," he had assured Sori.

To transform her dream into reality, Sori had decided to become a doctor, specializing in treating children's ailments. That meant, according to Dr. Sharif, she would have to become a pediatrician.

He would say, "My daughter, you have the *eshq*, the passion, and the intelligence to achieve your goals. I don't see any reason why you shouldn't be able to succeed." Then, he would quote Hafez:

Hargez namirad anke delash zenda shod ba eshq
Sabt ast bar jarida-e alam dawam-e ma
A heart alive with love will never die
Our immortality is inscribed in the journal of the universe

Sori had a destination in mind, and she had mapped out a clear path as to how to get there. Study hard, pass the university entrance exam, become a doctor. Then, open the health clinic. God willing, it will take about six to eight years to execute the plan. She had figured it all out.

Unfortunately, now there was no school from which she could graduate and move on to study medicine. Along with the school, Sarwar had torched her dreams as well, and she could do nothing to change that.

FOUR

Sori was born on a frosty winter morning. Two days prior to her birth, snow had started to fall and continued to come down without a break until a day after she was born. By then, a thick layer of heavy white powder had covered the unpaved Kamari Pass that linked the village to Kabul. On that day, a taxi and a Jeep had dared to embark on a journey from the city to the surrounding villages. However, soon after plowing through the main road for only a few yards, their chained tires remained entrapped and churning in the knee-high snow.

***

At dawn, Sekandar put on his worn-out jacket and walked to Qayoum Khan's *qala*, a high-walled compound. Khan was the only man in the village who could help him, and the only man on whom Sekandar could count. Khan had helped him numerous times in the past, and he would not hesitate to do the same again.

Shivering, Sekandar stood in the courtyard as cotton balls of snow landed on his black turban. He did not want to waste any more time than he had to by stepping up the stairs and entering the guestroom.

"I am in need of your kindness. I am about to lose Aziz's mother. I just don't know what to do," he said, skipping the normal exchange of pleasantries.

"What happened?" concerned, Qayoum Khan asked.

Desperation vibrated in Sekandar's voice, "The child is okay, but her mother is very sick." He was not able to stop his teeth from chattering.

Stepping down the stairs, Qayoum Khan wrapped his *pattu*, shawl around his torso. "Since when has this been going on?" His wife, Nafas Gul had told him that Mahro was expecting her third child anytime soon.

"It started around midnight."

"Why didn't you come earlier?" he looked surprised and a bit irritated.

"The child was okay. I thought she . . . would be okay too," Sekandar had hoped and prayed throughout the night that his wife would eventually stop bleeding.

Qayoum Khan looked up at the white winter sky and stared at it for a few seconds. Then, he turned around and called his wife, "Nafas Gul!" With his back toward Sekandar, he slipped his right hand into the side pocket of his vest. He then turned and slid his hand into the breast pocket of Sekandar's jacket, leaving ten crisp one hundred Afghani bills inside. "In case you need this," he said tapping on his chest. Once again, Qayoum Khan proved that he was indeed a true friend and a man of honor.

"People say, *roz-e bad biadar nadara*, the day of disaster has no brother. But I don't believe in that. May God bless you in return." Sekandar vowed to himself that should Qayoum Khan ever ask for help, he would not hesitate to sacrifice his own life for him.

***

Then, the small stature of Nafas Gul emerged from the dark corridor that led to the terrace.

"Salam Sekandar. Is everything okay? How is Mahro?"

"She is getting weaker by the minute, been losing too much blood, and burning with fever. Baby seems to be okay."

"God forbid, *nazar shoda*, she must have been ominously eyed. Let me put on my coat." She turned and disappeared back into the same hallway.

Qayoum Khan shouted, "Sekandar, don't waste time. Get Pekay," he was referring to the horse he had bought years ago during a hunting trip to Samangan province. "Go to Kabul, right now, and find a doctor. Bring him in a taxi. Leave the horse in Mandawi in the store next-door. Hurry man!"

Qayoum Khan owned a shop in the city's central market, where he sold his harvested products in bulk to shopkeepers around the city. Every year, Sekandar had been in charge of renting a truck and transferring the harvested corn from the farm, and flour from the mill to the store. Before Pekay's accident, sometimes he would ride the horse all the way to Kabul.

Failing to obey his command, Sekandar stared at Qayoum Khan Like a statue. He didn't even blink. Grief and confusion must have numbed the part of his brain responsible for making critical decisions.

"Sekandar, I am talking to you."

He jolted, as if awakening from a hypnotic dream, "Qayoum Khan, may you live a thousand years."

Taking brisk steps, Nafas Gul reappeared from the hallway. She was wearing a black coat and had slipped into her white snow boots. A pink cloth package, filled with various herbal medicines, dangled from her right hand.

"Don't worry. I'll take care of her," looking down at the package, she assured Sekandar. "God willing, my *Yunani*, Greek herbal medicine will cure her in no time.

***

Pekay rested, kneeling in a dark corner of the barn. A fistful of white hair was scattered over his forehead. He was charcoal-black without even a white speck on his body. Therefore, Sekandar had named him *Pekay*, The Bang.

"Come on boy, long journey ahead," he circled his arms around Pekay's neck and helped the aged animal stand on his feet.

During a brutal game of Buz-kashi in Samangan province eight years ago, an accident had left Pekay with a limping right foot. On that day, Sekandar had snatched the decapitated *buz*, goat from the opponent's hand and secured it on Pekay's back, ordering him to gallop on a slope toward the finishing circle, where they would drop the carcass and claim victory. But only a few yards before reaching their destination, the horse's right foot had sunk in a pothole undetectably covered by grass and weeds. Pekay, Sekandar, and the *buz* flew off in different directions, tumbling down the slope. Tossed by the impact of the violent jolt, the heavy carcass disjointed Sekandar's right elbow.

A few yards away, laying on the ground, Pekay could only lift his head, soaked in sweat. He could not rise and stand. Disabled by his broken right foot, he waited patiently for Sekandar to come to his rescue.

Not fully aware of his own injuries, Sekandar rose and sprinted toward the terrified animal. He raised and nestled his partner's head against his chest. Hot air flared through Pekay's nostrils. Meanwhile, he kept his wild-eyed gaze fixed on the ground, as though ashamed. He had failed to take his partner to the finish line.

***

Exiting the village, Sekandar passed by his own house. He thought of going inside to check on his wife. But that would cost him precious time. He had an idea as to what was going on inside. He could picture Mahro's unconscious body lying on the mattress, a faint, painful moan once every few minutes, blood, fever, more blood, and more fever gradually draining life out of her. Nothing could have changed, and he could do nothing to change the situation. Sekandar had to make it to Kabul, find a doctor, and bring him to the village as fast as he could. He decided to press on.

Sensing the urgency, Pekay paced with confidence. He knew the route to the city. He had traveled through the hills and valleys of the Kamari Pass many times. Now that he had found a second opportunity to help his partner reach the finish line, he was determined to do so. However, an hour later, still miles away from Kabul, his legs began to feel heavy, which made it more difficult and exhausting to push forward through the thick layer of snow. Nevertheless, he kept ambling on with slow but steady strides.

Sekandar realized that the horse was in trouble. He padded Pekay's back a couple of times, firm enough to keep him focused but not too strong to cause him pain. But Pekay maintained the same pace, laboring to breathe through his flaring nostrils and aging lungs. He had the drive, but not the strength to step any faster. Treating the old animal roughly would have been cruel, and it would not have helped him to pick up the pace either.

"Haaah! Move on son, move, faster!" frustrated, Sekandar shouted, but Pekay couldn't obey. He wanted to, he tried, but he just could not muster the energy to do it. In addition to the fact that his right front leg limped a little, years of inactivity and old age made it impossible for him to answer his partner's last call.

A few steps further, as the snow thickened and the road began to ascend, Pekay started to toddle along before coming to a complete halt. He hung his head low as puffs of his breath, like tiny patches of clouds, floated and disappeared in the sky. Sekandar studied the animal for a few seconds, then ran a hand on his black mane and planted a kiss on his forehead.

"Whatever His will," he said through a choked throat, lifting an index finger toward the overcast sky.

As he looked around, the colorless glare took a stab at his squinting eyes. Draped in a thick white comforter, the mountains remained deafeningly silent. Perhaps, under that spotless cloak they were concealing a dark secret from him.

He thought about Mahro, his childhood friend, one of the few literate women and the only redhead beauty in the village. Years ago, Mahro and her cousin, Nadia attended the same elementary school together in a nearby village. Mahro was much older and in a higher grade than Nadia. Nadia had moved on to the city, eventually graduating from Kabul University. Mahro, on the other hand, had remained in the village to marry the man she loved. Once her dream of marriage to the kind, polite, and handsome Sekandar came true, all she wanted was to stay in Deh Darya and raise her children alongside her husband.

***

O, God, don't take her from me. Sekandar pleaded, visualizing Mahro's dark-brown eyes, long eyelashes, and a heartwarming smile. *I need her. My kids need her. Please God! Let her live.*

Chunks of weightless snowflakes kept landing on the rocky mountain slopes, the giant boulders, and the barren branches of trees that extended like the claws of frozen monsters. Sekandar wrapped Pekay's rein around his wrist and stared at the rising path toward Kabul. Within a few hours, the sun will drift behind the mountains; everything white will turn gray, and eventually disappear in the dark. They had just begun to ascend the Kamari Pass. From thereon, it would take about five hours on a sunny day to walk to the city.

Would they make it to Kabul if they kept on climbing? Only God knew. If they did, for sure, it would be dark by the time they arrived. And if they didn't, the likelihood of their survival through the night would be slim.

Even if the snow decided to stop falling, and even if Sekandar found a doctor willing to walk to the village, it would not be possible to return in a taxi tomorrow. Sekandar was certain of that.

"I hope Nafas Gul's medicine works," he said to Pekay, his voice and his lips trembling.

Ashamed, Pekay kept his head down, waiting for him to make a decision.

Sekandar turned around and started to walk back toward Deh Darya. Pekay lurched along. As if the animal knew that next year, he would not be around to make up for this lost opportunity.

***

Arriving at the intersection between the main road and the path that led to the village, he noticed people entering his house in small groups. Once inside, he saw men huddling in the courtyard in clusters of three and four around the stripped rose shrubs. Qayoum Khan was the first to open his arms. Holding his friend in a gentle embrace, he whispered in Sekandar's ear with a sad tone, "May she rest in peace. May God grant you patience."

***

Sekandar raised the corner of the blanket that draped over the door-less frame of the guestroom's entrance. He dared not to step inside. Covered by a white cloth from head to toe, Mahro's lifeless body laid on the floor in the center of the room. Nafas Gul and about a dozen of Deh Darya's other women sat around her, weeping with puffy eyes and swollen nostrils. Shimmering from under the white cloth, a few strands of Mahro's red hair remained exposed. Sekandar let go of the curtain and pulled away from the doorway. He entered the other room across the squared entry area. Next to the window, his eight-year-old son, Aziz was sitting with his hands crossed around his folded knees and his face hidden in between. Holding the newborn near her chest, Nadia was sitting on the new rug that Mahro had bought just two weeks ago. Mahro had also stitched together a baby mattress, a small flat pillow, and a baby blanket as she had anticipated that her child would need to sleep through a harsh winter—this time, a girl as she had wished and prayed.

Nadia had failed to prevent the flow of her tears in the presence of Aziz, Jawad, and the baby. How could she? She had lost her best friend and her only cousin. Two-year-old Jawad sat next to her with rapidly blinking eyes and a confused expression on his face. "Baba! *Adey khaw ast*, Mommy is sleeping," he said pointing his little index finger toward the room across the hallway.

As tears blurred Sekandar's vision, he buried his face in his frozen hands.

FIVE

As the sun sunk behind the western mountain peaks, a chilly wind began to blow across the flat rooftop where Masih was sitting. Long shadows grew longer and hovered over the slopes.

Ready for ablution, Sekandar squatted in front of the exposed rose stems. Masih shouted to get his attention, "Baba, when are they coming back?"

"Any minute now. Be patient," he said, cupping the palms of his hands together for Sori to tilt the plastic jug and pour water on them. The glacial water from the well had melted off the Hindu Kush and purified itself traveling underground. When constructing his house, Sekandar had dug the deepest well in the village in a corner of his front yard. Its depth and proximity to the river just across the street, helped maintain a sizeable reservoir of water. Even if the river dried out in hot summers, Deh Darya never faced a shortage of drinking water. Sekandar's well could quench the thirst of the entire village.

He never performed ablution with warm water, not even in winters. "Hot water is for *bachaa-e shir o parata*, milk and honey boys," he would say. Sori made every effort to pour the exact amount on his hands, just enough—no more, no less.

As she tipped the pitcher, Masih could not help but notice the glitter of the chiseled glass bangles sliding on her milky-white forearms. Her headscarf rested on her shoulders, exposing a cascade of charcoal-black hair to a playful gust of wind. Masih did not resist the temptation. In fact, he took advantage of the opportunity and enjoyed watching her from the safety of the secluded rooftop. However, within a few seconds, feelings of shame and regret shot through his mind. True, Sori was stunning, and it would not have been easy for any fourteen-year-old boy to ignore her. Still, that did not give him the right to stare at her in that manner.

As guilt weighed heavy on his mind, he dropped his eyes to the edge of the rooftop. He felt embarrassed of committing a *be-ghairati*, a dishonorable act. After all, he had been friends with Sori's brothers for as long as he could remember. Plus, he spent the first two years of his life living with Sori in the same house. So what if he couldn't recall any memories of her from that time? So what if he was just an infant back then? It didn't change the fact that, for however short a period, they were raised together as brother and sister in the same household. As far as she was concerned, they were siblings, and everyone else thought so too.

Maybe this time he made a mistake—a disgraceful one. It just was not right to have inappropriate feelings for his best friends' sister, and it should not occur ever again. When Sori's brothers treated Masih's mother as a sister, it would not be fair for him to think of their sister as anything but a sister. A burst of heat rushed through his body. He released his sweaty palms from the edge of the rooftop and pulled back. Then he dusted off his knees, hoping to avoid his mother's criticism for ruining his only pair of jeans that was almost an inch short around his ankles.

Masih walked toward the pigeon coop and sat next to its fenced door, only a foot higher than his waistline. He pulled his knees close to his chest and gazed into the dark chamber. On the opposite side, a golden ray of sunlight shimmered through the fenced window that opened toward Baba's garden behind the house. Cool and depressing shadows dominated inside the structure that was neither a cage, nor a room. Facing each other, the pigeons sat on two wooden rods, which hung from the ceiling with metal wires twisted around each end. As usual, the doves patiently waited for the brothers to arrive and let them out.

He could identify a few of the pairs as Aziz and Jawad had taught him—*Caasa-dum, Siah-patain, Sabz-shirazi, and Malaqi.* As he looked closer, there drifted a new pair toward the end of the rod, right next to the small opening in the wall. While others fidgeted and muttered a "coo, coo," the newcomers kept quiet and almost motionless, as if they were lost deep in thoughts. Masih had seen the likes of them flying around the shrine of Sakhi-jan in Kabul. Since Father's disappearance, he and Mother would visit the shrine at least twice a month to pray for him and supplicate for his return.

A few minutes later, he stood up and headed for *bala-khana*, the upper room on the opposite corner of the rooftop. Waiting for Aziz and Jawad's arrival, he could sit there on a mattress, listen to the river surge, and watch the berry trees rock. But before entering the room, he shot a final glance at the wooden bridge across the river, and for the first time he saw armed *mujahedin,* fighters crossing it. Masih was pleasantly surprised.

SIX

Kalashnikovs, the same machineguns that the Soviet soldiers carried around, slung over Aziz and Jawad's shoulders and rounds of bullets, attached to leather straps, crisscrossed their chests. A pistol hung from one hip, a *qama*, a double-edged dagger from the other, and another ammunition belt lined with magazines wrapped around their waists. With sunburned, bearded faces and soiled traditional clothes, much baggier than what people normally wore, they looked similar to how Masih had pictured the *mujahedin* fighters.

***

Sori entered the upper room, holding a tray that contained a plate with cookies, four cups, and a china kettle filled with green tea.

"Salam Lala. Tea?" out of respect, Jawad and Sori called Aziz *Lala*, big brother—and so did the rest of the youth in Deh Darya.

"Yes, God bless you," Aziz laid his weapon against the wall, in the corner near the doorway. Jawad's weapon leaned right next to it. The brothers piled their belts, magazines, handguns, and daggers in the same corner. Then, they slouched on two mattresses across from each other and leaned their sore backs against the pillows.

"How did it go?" Sekandar sat crisscrossed on another mattress under the window, turning his prayer beads in between his wrinkled, dry fingers. Almost every evening he would sit there with his eyes shut meditating, mumbling verses from the Holy Quran, and waiting for his sons to return from the mountains.

"The same," Aziz answered, "we're almost prepared for a big operation, one of these days, God willing."

Sarwar and his men returned from Pakistan three weeks ago. Since their arrival, they had spent every single day, preparing dugouts and barricades on the rocky hills that overlooked the main road along the river. The brothers possessed skills and strength that came in handy when digging hideouts and moving rocks around. After all, they extracted, smashed, and hauled rocks for a living—sometimes using explosives, other times with just a pickaxe and a sledgehammer.

Sarwar and his men believed that after the project was completed, it would make it harder for any Soviet convoy to pass through the Tangi valley. Once the *mujahedin* inflicted heavy casualties on the Soviets and their puppets, they would not dare to cross that road again.

***

Masih stood by the doorway, staring at the pile of ammunition and weapons. He wondered how it would feel to carry a machinegun, a modern weapon that he had only seen in World War II movies at Baharestan Cinema. Sekandar raised his teacup with one hand, and with the other beckoned Masih, "Come *Jan-e Baba*, Baba's dear, sit next to me." He tapped on the mattress where he was sitting, only a couple of feet from the pile of weapons.

In addition to the two Kalashnikovs, there was one other weapon in the room. A rifle, called Jezail hung from two nails on the wall opposite the doorway. Baba had inherited the gun from his grandfather, who had passed it on to his son. Masih had touched and held that rifle a couple of years ago. He remembered his arms succumbing under its weight within a few seconds. It would be nice if he could hold a Kalashnikov too. Was it heavier than a Jezail? Would he be able to walk around the mountains with one slung over his shoulder when he became a *mujahed*, fighter? Would he be able to lift the weapon up to shoot the enemy? It would have been nice to know the answer to those questions. But first, he must find a way to become a fighter.

"How long have you been a *mujahed*, Lala Aziz?"

"I have always been a fighter. *Jihad*, the struggle is in my blood. I have inherited it from my grandfathers," he said, alluding to his great grandfather's participation in the first and second Anglo-Afghan wars, and his grandfather's participation in the third war against the British. Baba had told him that both men, grandpa and great-grandpa were sharp shooters and fearless warriors. Grandfather had not been born yet, when his father was killed in the battlefield. Therefore, they never saw each other, but they lived nearly identical lives, and died in the same manner—martyred by the infidels. Now, Aziz and Jawad had an opportunity to achieve the same honor as their ancestors.

"Mulla Salim says it's our *farz-ul Ayn*, essential religious duty to fight against the invaders, just like our grandfathers did," Jawad said.

"Yep, they defeated an empire, we'll beat a superpower. Be it *Englis*, Britain or *Shorawi*, Russia, they are all the same," Aziz said.

"*Sag-e zard, biadar-e shaghl*, yellow dog, the brother of a jackal." Baba never missed an opportunity to state a proverb related to the subject of a conversation. Everyone laughed except for Masih. He had witnessed the Soviets' military might. *These men don't know what they are up against*, he thought to himself.

"So, when the Soviets roll in with their tanks, how are you going to fight them?" Masih asked.

"We are not scared of their tanks. God willing, we'll shred them into pieces," Aziz said.

Jawad raised the palm of his hand toward the ceiling, "We don't care about their machines. We want to deal with the guys operating them."

Masih said, "This Kalashnikov is so small. It is not even going to make a hole in a tank."

"This thing fires about a hundred bullets a minute. It is a lethal weapon." Aziz leaned over and picked up the Kalashnikov, "Here, check it out."

Surprised and pleased, Masih accepted his offer with a grin plastered on his face. As he let go, Masih's arms sunk under the weight of the weapon. No doubt, it was heavier than the Jezail. Judging by its appearance and weight, it must be capable of inflicting some serious damage to whomever or whatever it hit. It would definitely cause more harm than the Jezail did. Still, Masih could not see how in the world a small weapon like that could shoot down a flying dragon. Besides, despite its impressive look and feel, firing that weapon at a tank would be like throwing pebbles at an elephant.

While pretending, without much success, that he had no trouble handling the weapon, he raised it and ran his fingers along its barrel and stock, "Lala, I have seen a tank, and the *charkhaki*, helicopter too. If you fired at them with one of these machineguns, they wouldn't even feel it. I am sorry, but I am just not convinced that you could beat the Soviets with this."

Aziz said, "Well, next time Sarwar travels to Pakistan, he'll get us some heavy weapons, mortars, launchers, those sorts of things. Then, we will make the bears run like mice."

Jawad said, "To be honest, I don't even care. If they have technology, we have God on our side. Let me put it this way. We fulfil our duty to God and to this country. If we live, we are *Ghazi*, a soldier of God, and if they kill us, we are *Shahid*, a martyr. Either way we win; we go to paradise."

Baba nodded his head in agreement, "You are right son, but remember, according to *Sharia*, Islamic law, protecting oneself is every Muslim's duty."

"Yes, Baba," said Jawad obediently.

"I've heard enough. Let me see how tough this machinegun of yours is," Baba extended his hand and reached for the weapon sitting in Masih's lap.

Unsuccessful in making the act appear effortless, Masih held the weapon up and offered it to Baba.

Using only one hand, Baba clutched the Kalashnikov as if snatching a feather in the air. That was the second surprise of the day for Masih. As far back as he could remember, Baba executed every task slowly and with much deliberation, and no one could blame him for that. The man was probably ninety or one hundred years old, or maybe he just appeared to be old. Nobody really knew his age, including himself. Baba never seemed to be in a hurry. He took his time walking, eating, speaking, and even breathing. But age alone did not slow him down. His decade-old back injury, which had never entirely healed, also affected his mobility.

To face the open window, Baba made a one-eighty turn, raised the Kalashnikov, and pushed its butt against his right shoulder. Impressed by his agility, Masih detected a slight quiver in his right hand as he reached for the trigger.

"This feels like a plastic toy," he flashed a smile at Masih.

Masih responded with a grin of his own. For about ten seconds, Baba held one eye shut, and the other on the sight, his quivering index finger wrapped around the trigger. Across from his house, birds of all sorts took refuge on the berry trees. The chill of the plundering wind from the mountains kept them huddled on the revived branches. With budding blossoms and leaves, the trees had just awakened from a long dormancy period.

A cool gust whistled through the room and exited through the opposite window that opened toward the garden, yet nothing moved. The sun, surrounded by haphazard dark blue clouds along with orange and red streaks crisscrossing the gray sky, was about to sink behind the mountains.

Is he going to shoot a bird? Like a wedding drum, his heart pounded. A poor bird looking forward to a season of joy and excitement was about to perish and miss the chance to fly tomorrow—on the first day of spring. *Please don't!* He almost blurted.

"Relax. I won't shoot," Baba said releasing the trigger and turning toward Masih, as if he had heard him plea. Then he stood up, returned the Kalashnikov to the corner of the room, and stepped toward the Jezail.

Holding its crescent-shaped stock with one hand and its long barrel with the other, Sekandar kissed the rifle and rubbed the palm of his hand over its stock. The only other item that his sons had seen him kiss and handle with such reverence was the Holy Quran. After all, that weapon laid next to his grandfather when he was martyred.

"This is the real deal," he held it up over his head like an athlete raising a trophy.

"That gun was good for its own time. In today's war, it's just not going to do the job," Jawad said.

"My son, this gun has defeated the Brits," Sekandar said, shaking the rifle upright to emphasize its significance. "What has your Kalashnikov done so far?"

"Baba, by the time you load up the Jezail, a Kalashnikov would have already fired fifty rounds," Aziz said nodding toward the corner where the weapons were stocked.

"Well, the Jezail has already passed its test; not once, but three times. It deserves our utmost respect. When your Kalashnikov kicks the Soviets out of Afghanistan, you can brag about it too," Baba did not seem convinced at all by his son's argument.

"God willing, that will happen soon; maybe next year," Aziz said.

Next year was going to be tomorrow. Masih would wear his new traditional Afghan clothes on *Nawroz*, the New Year's Day, and pray in the mosque. He will listen to Mulla Salim's first *khotba*, sermon of the year. According to Father, Salim was a fearless mulla.

SEVEN

After reciting Quranic verses and wishing everyone a happy and blessful new year, Mulla Salim opened his speech with a line from Hafez, the 14th century poet:

Faash megoyam o azgofta-e khoddelshaadam
Barda-e eshqam o az har do jahan azaadam
I bluntly disclose the truth and am pleased with what I say
I am enslaved by love and free from both worlds

"Dear Muslim brothers, it is my religious duty to tell you the truth, and tell it bluntly and in simple words. Infidelity, that's what this Godless regime is all about. It is based on denial of God and disrespect for the believer. Communists equate religion with opium as an obstruction to human sanity and society, but we believe that religion is our way of life. That's why Islam and Communism oppose each other, and can never coexist.

Salim was no more than five feet-three inches tall. The height of the black turban on his head did not help to make him appear any taller either, and his baggy clothes made his scrawny physique look even smaller. He had darkened his tiny brown eyes with *surma*, kohl. Between those shiny marbles stood a thin nose. The wrinkles around his eyes revealed that his youth had left him years ago. However, not even one white strand could be seen in his neatly trimmed beard. He must have dyed it, Masih thought.

"The Marxists claim that their religion will bring *beradari*, brotherhood, and *barabari*, equality among Afghans. Let me tell you, Islam introduced these ideals to the world more than a thousand years ago." Aside from the creases pressed by an iron, no other crinkle was visible on Mulla Salim's outfit. Every time he gestured with his hands, his sleeves slipped down to his elbows and revealed the silver band of his watch. It reminded Masih of the chains of the Soviet tanks rolling on the streets of Kabul.

"Sharia itself is a complete law. Equality, freedom, and justice are all Islamic values. I don't need the communists to teach me those lessons. Then, brothers, I ask you: Why should I abandon God and instead worship Lenin?" A few of the men chuckled, others whispered, exchanging comments with each other.

"Today, nobody asks why so many of our youth have converted to Communism. Why they have turned away from God? Why are they selling their *namoos*, honor to the Soviets?" Even though the mulla spoke fluent Dari, now and then a slight Pashto accent would surface in his low-pitched voice. He spoke loudly, yet with a soft and slow tone. Then, he paused to allow the worshipers ponder the questions. Silence weighed heavy in the atmosphere.

"Because," he proceeded to answer his own questions, "they are all educated in *Shorawi*, the Soviet Union. It is not that they are trained in one or two days. The Soviets are brainwashing our kids, injecting infidelity into innocent youths' minds," Mulla Salim turned his eyes from the far left to the far right to ensure that he had the attention of every single soul present.

Except for a cough or two, the legacy of a long and harsh winter, no other sound could be heard, as if the crowd had gone into a hypnotic trance. Nobody moved. Not only had the charm in mulla's voice captured the audience's attention, the clarity in his speech, and the boldness of his claims held his audience captive. They seemed to have no other choice but to listen and stare.

At least, thirty rows of worshipers stretched from one end of the prayer house to the other. Everybody sat on the floor. Despite his small size, sitting on the top step of the pulpit, Salim towered over his audience.

Masih was sitting next to Sekandar, who sat beside his old friend, Qayoum Khan. On his right, Qari Abdulla, Mulla Salim's only son was kneeling down. In the mosque, he was in charge of making the daily calls for prayers five times a day. At age twelve, Abdulla had already earned the title of *qari*, one who recites the holly book from memory. Small in stature like his father, he recited the Quranic verses with a powerful and melodic tone.

As tradition mandated, the elders occupied the rest of the first row on both sides. Masih and Abdulla were the only boys sitting at the front, because one was Baba's guest, and the other was a *qari*.

Men from far and near villages had come to pray in Deh Darya's mosque, just to listen to Mulla Salim's speech. Worshipers who arrived late and could not fit inside the mosque, sat on their own praying mats and shawls out in the courtyard. Speaking loud, Mulla Salim made sure that they too could hear him.

Among the many attendees, a government spy or two must have been listening somewhere inside or outside the mosque. That meant Mulla Salim's provocative speech was in fact nothing short of a suicide attempt.

Every few minutes, a breeze would blow in through the three large windows that faced the river, and whoosh out through the other three windows opening on the opposite side toward the cornfields. The sound of flowing water and the clamor of the birds resonated in the background. Even though the windows remained wide open, the varied scents of cheap colognes hung in the atmosphere. Two years ago, while exiting the same mosque after a Friday prayer, Masih had complained to Father about the smell. Father had laughed and told him that it was the "fragrance" of cheap cologne and aftershave imported from Pakistan.

Like Qayoum Khan, Mulla Salim inherited many acres of land bordering that of Qayoum Khan's. He had also inherited the duties of his father in the mosque. Salim's father had led prayers from the same spot where now he was delivering the *Khotba*, sermon. Both men were mullas. However, Salim had graduated from Kabul University's Faculty of Religious Studies, while his father had gone through only a year of religious education in a Pakistani *madrasa*, religious school.

Salim went on to say, "Therefore, it is my duty to invite you to join our brave *mujahed* sons of this country in their struggle against injustice and foreign invasion. This war is not just about our country. It's about our religion, values, traditions. Our national identity is at risk. And *jihad* is not my call. It's an order from God." Then, he recited a verse from the Holy Quran, "*Fight them on until there is no more tumult or oppression.*' So, if you are an adult who is able to fight, join the *mujahedin* in their struggle to restore the rule of God in Afghanistan. Let's show the infidels that we are the sons of the same fathers who defeated the *Farangi*, the Westerners. And if you don't have the *ghairat*, honor to be a *mujahed*, fighter, or whatever your reason is, don't cooperate with the infidels either. As God almighty says, '*Whomever takes them as friends, is indeed from them.*' We are famous in hospitality around the world. Aren't we?" he paused. "Then let's show the Soviets some hospitality." He cleared his throat, and recited a lyric from a famous song by Ustad Qasem, which Masih had heard on the radio a while ago:

Gar nadani ghairat-e Afghani-am
Choon ba maidanamadi medani-am
If you don't understand my Afghan honor
Once you come to the battleground, you will

Hearing his sarcastic remark, followed by the timely insertion of a provocative lyric, his audience seemed moved, nodding their heads in affirmation.

"The second point I want to make is this: Don't send your children to schools in Kabul, where the communists corrupt them. Yes, they should be educated—learning is every Muslim's duty, but not learning blasphemy. Bring them to the mosque. *I* will educate them."

Mulla Salim's statement brought back yesterday's memory of Sori's tearful eyes. Had she been among the audience, she would have definitely refuted his claim that school will corrupt children. Without a doubt, she would have stood up in that room crowded with men, and told the Mulla that he was wrong. Masih knew this because she had seen her in action before. When Sori had a point, she would make it, arguing against anybody, anytime.

She is just like her mother, God bless her soul, feisty and stubborn. He had heard Mother say numerous times after an argument or a long discussion with her.

Everyone knew that a year prior to her death, Mahro had marched right into the mosque and passionately argued with Mulla Salim. She had accused him of being unfairly strict toward women. Salim had issued a decree, prohibiting women of Deh Darya from traveling to Kabul without a *chadari*, burqa or a male companion. He had contended that Kabul had become the bastion of impiety and immorality. Therefore, women should protect themselves by wearing a burqa when traveling to the city.

Mahro had argued that she was an Afghan and a village woman tough enough to beat up any Kabuli man, should he dare to look at her with a bad eye. *God is with me. I don't need the veil or a man to protect me,* she had argued.

Now, had Mahro's daughter been there, she too would have bluntly told Mulla Salim that he was dead wrong. *Thank God, she is not here,* Masih said to himself. *Maybe it is a good thing that women aren't allowed to pray together with men in the mosque.*

***

Soon after the prayer, as everyone rose to say Happy New-Year to each other, village elders flocked around Qayoum Khan, Baba, and Mulla Salim.

"You know Masih, Dr. Sharif's son?" Baba introduced him to the elders. Some would say, *Pir shawi,* may you grow old my son. I pray for your father five times a day." Recognizing Dr. Sharif's sacrifice, they welcomed his son with a firm handshake and an attitude that implied respect and gratitude.

Masih bowed and kissed the back of elders' hands, answering with a polite *Salam,* hello, yes, and thank you. Among them, Mulla Salim surprised him with a powerful handshake. "We are proud of your father. Remember, you are the son of a true hero."

An instant surge of pride rushed through Masih. Too bad Father wasn't there to see how much people loved and respected him.

***

Outside the mosque, Aziz, Jawad, and a few other bearded boys huddled around Sarwar. He stood out among the crowd with a torso as wide as a blackberry tree and a neck as thick as the rubber bucket with which Sori drew water from the well. The overarch of his brows, the fierce expression on his chubby face, long hair curling out from under his hat, and an unkempt beard did not make him appear approachable.

They wore either a grey turban or a hat, as if they all had shopped from the same store. Their tan, grey, or olive vests, with numerous pockets on each side looked alike as well.

***

"We are going home to let the pigeons out," Jawad said, "want to join us?"

"Sure," Masih was happy to leave the scene without having to greet Sarwar. He didn't like his arrogant attitude to begin with. Now, after hearing what he had done to Sori's school, he dreaded even saying hello to him.

As he stepped outside the mosque, he noticed two fighters armed with Kalashnikovs standing guard on each side of the gate. Four other machineguns leaned against the wall where the guards were standing.

"Just make sure to be on time for lunch," Said Qayoum Khan as Sekandar, Mulla Salim, and Qari Abdulla joined him in walking toward his compound.

***

"What a brave man, what a speech! This guy knows no fear," Jawad said as they walked next to the river toward home.

"I agree with the things he said, but with these kinds of words he will get himself and us in trouble," Aziz said.

"The government is not going to touch him. Salim is the most famous and respected Mulla in the region. I like him. He is a cool and *ghairati*, honorable guy."

"Yes, but spies are everywhere, and he knows that."

"Then why does he say all these things?" Masih jumped in, trying to keep up with the pace.

"I think he says these things on purpose," Said Aziz.

"Why would he do that?" Masih asked.

"I bet he wants the government to come after him."

"Are you saying he has lost his mind?"

42

"No, he hasn't lost his mind. He is thinking. He wants to do two things; get the people to stand up against the government, and to become a hero, a leader, even a martyr."

Jawad asked, "How do you know?"

"I don't. I am just guessing, and I think I am right."

"But if he becomes a martyr, who is going to spread his word?"

"His martyrdom, his reputation is going to do that. Everybody will talk about him for many years. He has a lot of followers, you know. They will always think of him as a hero, and more people will join the fight just to avenge his blood," Aziz said.

"That's brave, but kind of crazy," Masih said.

"To you it is. To him it makes perfect sense."

"Well, whatever the mulla's plans are, after listening to him, I can't wait to find a Soviet base and attack it—right now," Jawad made a fist and hurled it toward the sky.

"Yeah," Masih punched the air too.

They took a few more steps in silence before Masih said what he had wanted to say since after the arrest of his father, "I want to be a *mujahed*. If Mother let me stay with you guys, would you teach me how to fight?"

"Of course we will. You don't know how to fire a weapon, do you?" Aziz asked.

"Not really, but I can learn. I know how to hold a gun," he sounded confident.

"That's good, but I don't think your mother will let you stay with us. You know how she feels about your school. And without her permission, you are not allowed to fight."

Jawad agreed, "He's right. We had to get permission from Baba too. Luckily, we didn't have to beg."

"I don't understand. Why wouldn't she let me fight for my country?"

"Masih, it's not time for you to become a fighter," Aziz said.

"Why not? I am a Muslim, an Afghan. It's my duty too."

"True, but you also have other obligations that come first."

"What could be more important?"

"At your age, your duty is to learn and take care of your mother."

"I can't just go to school and watch the Soviets gobble up Afghanistan. I want to be a real *mujahed*, a warrior like you guys."

"I know you do. Maybe one day you will be one."

"Well, if school is so important, then why did you guys set it on fire?"

"We didn't. Sarwar did," Jawad said. "In fact, we tried to change his mind. We told him that kids need to learn something; people will hate us for doing that. But he didn't listen."

"Jawad is right. We had nothing to do with the school burning. If anything, we tried to stop him. But Sarwar is the commander, and he is Qayoum Khan's son, you know," Aziz said.

"If I become a *mujahed*, I won't do anything like that. My goal is to kick the Soviets out of Afghanistan. You see, the faster they are gone, the sooner Father will come home. That's why I have to be a *mujahed*."

Jawad turned his teary eyes away toward the river.

"Listen," Aziz stopped walking, "you do your part, we do ours. Leave the fighting to us. Right now, your biggest job is to make sure your mother is okay. She has nobody but you."

Aziz's mini-speech reminded Masih of the very last words that Father had told him: *Take care of your mother. Always obey her, and finish school.*

Reluctantly, he nodded.

Groups of women and children were approaching from the opposite direction, wearing their colorful *Nawrozi*, New Year's dresses. They were returning from their visit to the cemetery, where they prayed for their lost loved ones. The brothers walked up to their mother's grave, raised their hands and prayed. Masih also held his hands up in prayer, asking God to bless aunt Mahro's soul, and to bring his father home.

***

"Here, you let them out," Aziz held a key, his hand stretched toward Masih.

That was the first time that he had offered him the key to the dove-house. Not even Jawad could unlock the door in his Lala's presence.

Surprised, Masih gladly accepted the offer and after a brief struggle, unlocked the fenced door. The doves began stirring on the wooden bars. Seeing Masih, some panicked, others seemed restless. In the end, it took less than a minute for the birds to hop out of the cage and begin to groom their feathers and stretch their wings. At first, all of them looked somewhat alike. But variation in feather colors and arrangements made each pair unique. Hence, a specific name was assigned to them. Could the white doves have a particular name for their type? Masih raised the question. It turned out that they actually did have a category—*Kaghazi*, Paper White according to Jawad.

"Don't keep them waiting," Aziz said.

Understanding what he meant, Masih formed a circle with his right thumb and index finger and pushed it under his curled up tongue. Next, he pulled as much air as he could into his lungs and blew it out through his teeth. The whistle pierced through the valley, and the surprised look on the brothers' faces assured him that indeed he had learned how to whistle.

The pigeons flapped their wings and took off flying in a circle above the house, above the river, and higher than the highest branches of the berry trees. A minute later, it seemed as though they were flying even farther and higher than the mountain peaks. Perhaps, it just looked that way because the mountains lay in the background far from the village. The doves kept circling in the boundless sky, a playground in which to enjoy those few precious moments of freedom.

"*Wah, wah*, bravo, you have learned how to whistle," Jawad said.

"Thanks to you."

"What about me?" Aziz frowned.

"You too, I guess," Masih said smiling.

A few months ago, during his visit to Deh Darya, Jawad had worked with him on his whistling skills. To demonstrate, circling his thumb and index finger under his tongue, he had executed the whistle a dozen times. Masih had tried emulating him repeatedly, but with no success at all. Not a single sound, just an empty blow. Then Aziz had stepped in, offering a few tips of his own, "Look, keep your fingers together, your tongue really has to be curled back, like this, you see? Push as hard as you can."

Masih listened and tried the trick. But to his dismay, no result. Then, he tried again, and again in a series of failed attempts, but he did not give up. After leaving the village, immediately he began to practice. *Try hard and be patient.* He remembered Father's advice. So, he kept practicing on the way to Kabul in Khalifa Zaman's bus. He practiced at home, and tried to whistle in school during recess and back at home again—more than just a few dozen times.

Then, after about a week, once every ten tries or so, he could hear a sound somewhat like a whistle thrusting through his teeth. Encouraged, he continued to try, even though his mouth had dried up and his tongue felt swollen. He kept trying and remained patient just as Father had advised. Finally, Mother complained that his whistles were too loud and he needed to go in the backyard to practice. It was then when Masih realized that he had learned how to whistle.

Every time the doves flew out for a spin, they had returned to the rooftop, jumping right back into the dove house; not even once had they failed to return. They could have headed for the mountains, or sat on a berry tree across the street like the other birds. But they didn't; they always returned home. Why would they want to come back time after time, only to be locked in? Why would they simply not fly away? Certainly, Jawad and Aziz couldn't grow wings to fly after them. Masih had to ask.

"Where would they go? They have no place to run to," Aziz said, jumping over the flat rooftop of the dove-house. He sat there with his feet dangling.

"They can go anywhere they want. Once they fly away, nobody can catch them," Masih said.

"See, that's what you don't understand. They can't just fly anywhere."

"Why is that?"

"Because they are used to living like this," Jawad said.

Aziz looked up. His eyes followed the flock completing yet another circle, "They have lived all of their lives in the dove house. They are used to it."

"Don't they want to be free?"

"They don't know what freedom is. When I bought them from *Bazaar-e Kaah-Foroshi*, they were in a cage. I brought them home in a cardboard box, and since then they have always been locked up."

"Yep, that's what captivity does to you. After a while, it makes you forget all about freedom," Aziz said. Then, he recited the line from Ahmad Zaher's famous song:

Zendagi akher sar ayad, bandagi dar kar nest
Bandagi gar shart bashad, zendagi dar kar nest
Eventually, life will end, slavery is not an option

If slavery is the condition, life is not an option

Jawad said, "Remember, we are not enslaving them. We just want them to be happy and alive. All this time we have been taking care of them. Now they don't know how to take care of themselves."

"Even if you feed me kabob every day, I won't spend a second in that cage," Masih said, pointing at the dove house.

A grin formed on Jawad's skinny bearded face, "It's because to you freedom tastes better than kabob."

Smiling, Aziz said, "But if you knew that the cat was going to eat you, I don't think you would have minded spending a night in there."

Referring to his own and Masih's green eyes, Jawad said, "Masih and I are cats ourselves. He is a city cat and I am a country cat."

They burst into laughter. Aziz bent down while laughing, and held his hands on his stomach. When the laughter subsided, Masih said, "Maybe they are simply loyal. Maybe they don't leave because they like you guys."

"Maybe, but actually not all of them are as loyal as you think," having gained his composure, Aziz said. "Just last month, a *Siah-Patain* pair parted way with the flock. We never saw them again."

Jawad said, "I told the boys that if our doves get mixed up with anybody's flock, bring them back."

"I don't want anybody's charity. Why did you say that?" Aziz said while drawing a cloth bag filled with birdseed from one of his vest's pockets.

"I didn't ask for charity," Jawad shot back with a defensive tone. "I was asking for what's *already* ours."

"Once a dove is gone, it's gone forever," Aziz opened the thread tied around the seed bag, and scattered a fistful of its contents on the rooftop. Then, he offered it to Masih, "You want to try?"

"Of course," Masih poured a fistful of seeds on his palm and began dispersing it in different directions, "Bih, Bih, Bih . . ."

At first, the doves seemed uninterested, but he insisted on scattering around even bigger fistfuls. At last, they stalled, and in spiraling circles that diminished in circumference descended on the rooftop. As the birds enjoyed the feast, Aziz's mind drifter far from Deh Darya, to an unknown place, where Fatima, the girl of his dreams lived—somewhere out there. He cleared his throat, shut his eyes and began humming:

Kujayi dilbar-e shirin-e ashiq?
Kujayi ay gul-e Sori-e ashiq?
Where are you, o my sweetheart?
Where are you, o my vibrant flower?

He sang with a well-impersonated Hazaragi accent, his voice did not resemble that of the actual singer's, Safdar Tawakoli. However, that is not to say he couldn't carry a tune. The sincerity and the burn in his voice testified to how much he cared about and missed Fatima, Sori's best friend.

Usually, when Fatima saw Aziz, her first reaction would be to hold a corner of her green scarf in between her teeth, smile, and turn around, perhaps because she was shy, or because she loved to show off her braided hair extending all the way down to her waistline. And when she pretended to be tidying her skirt, even though it draped neatly below her knees, a cherry glow flashed on her round smiling face.

At the same time, entering the front yard and realizing that Fatima had come to see Sori, Aziz would keep his gaze fixed on the ground as if he was looking for a lost item. The man who walked with the grace of a lion would act like a kitten in Fatima's presence. He had no doubt that Sori had sensed an awkward discomfort between them. He had also noticed that Fatima's reaction had been accompanied by a smile, which meant that she probably liked him. Therefore, Aziz decided to ask Sori to talk to Fatima to learn about her opion of him.

He would ask her to do that for sure, some day, one of these days. *If she agrees, can you please go to her house for khastgari,* proposal? He would just put it out there, simple and painless. It shouldn't be that complicated. Fatima either likes him, which she most likely does, or he could have misinterpreted her smile, in which case it would be 'a little' embarrassing.

Either way, he was willing to take the risk for the reward of making Fatima his wife. Would there be any reason for him to receive a negative response? Aziz could not think of one. And what about Baba? Will he object? Of course, Sori would have to get his permission prior to putting on her new dress and heading for

Fatima's house. There was no reason for Baba to oppose the marriage. He knew that Fatima was a well-mannered girl. Plus, Aziz had never heard him say anything negative about Hazara or Shia people. He himself was a Pashtun who did not speak Pashto. Occasionally, he would mumble a *Szenga ye*, how are you, and that was pretty much about it.

Hazara, Pashtun, Shia, Sunni. This stuff is all nonsense. We are humans, period. He had heard his father say on a few occasions.

Alas, Aziz was unaware that Fatima would soon leave and go to an unknown place, another village, or maybe a big city far from Deh Darya.

But, departing the village was not her idea. One day, her father, Mehdi Agha walked into the room where Fatima, her mother and brother, Reza sat having lunch. "Reza's mother," he said referring to his wife, "we need to start packing. We are leaving the day after tomorrow."

He had announced his decision three days after the miraculous return of the seventeen-year-old Reza. A month ago, *talashi*, the Afghan National Army's recruiting unit had kidnapped Reza. Their job was to snatch teenage boys off the streets of Kabul and enlist them into the military. Reza had forgotten to put his student I.D. in his pocket prior to leaving the house for Kabul. Without it, he had no proof of his status as a student. Therefore, on that day he was not exempt from military service. A week after his disappearance though, he was able to escape from *Kandak-e Tajjamo*, the Draftee Assembly Center. Finally, after a six-hour walk and run, he had made it back home.

Reza's father had explained the situation to his wife and daughter, "This time he ran away. What will we do when they take him again? I don't have money to bribe people. We can't take this chance again."

The night prior to her departure to Iran, Fatima could not shut her eyes and sleep, not even for a second. She watched the moon, the same moon that Aziz was watching through the window of the upper room.

That morning, Fatima went to Baba's house to say goodbye to her friend and perhaps see Aziz for the last time.

"Excuse me?" Sori had been shocked, hearing the news, "I'm not going to let my future sister-in-law leave the village."

49

"Maybe it wasn't God's will. I hope you find yourself a better sister-in-law. Say goodbye to Aziz for me. I will never forget you guys," Fatima sounded as if she knew she would never return to Deh Darya.

Aziz was nowhere to be found. He had gone to the mountain.

***

As Masih scattered the last fistful of seeds, Aziz said, "They had their lunch. Now it's our turn."

One by one, the doves scampered into the coop. Masih locked the screen door and followed the brothers climbing down the stairs.

They headed for Qayoum Khan's compound, where Noor's famous *qabeli-palaw,* a combination of rice, carrots, raisins, beef and nuts was about to be served. Food was all Masih could think of, not knowing that he was about to discover a secret, a truth that would kill his appetite.

EIGHT

The aroma of *qabeli-palaw* filled the atmosphere around Qayoum Khan's house. Armed with a Kalashnikov, the man who stood guard behind the high wall of the compound shook hands with Aziz and Jawad. "Happy New Year," he said with a somber look on his face.

In front of the gate, on the damp ground children played with marbles. A group of teenage boys, who seemed a year or two older than Masih, stood across the dusty path, pushing and shoving each other and once every few seconds bursting into a laughter. As they saw Aziz and Jawad approaching along with the skinny city boy, they stood almost motionless and forgot all about jokes and laughter.

"*Salam*. May you not be tired," they addressed the brothers, placing their right hand on their heart with a slight bow of the head.

"*Alaikum Salam*," Aziz stepped forward and shook everybody's hand. Jawad and Masih followed his lead.

One of the boys, the short stocky one, worked up the courage to say, "Happy New Year."

"Happy New Year to you too, Akram," Aziz said. "You look very strong, like a wrestler. One of these days, we'll have to figure out who is stronger between the two of us."

The idea sounded ridiculously absurd. Everyone laughed, and so did Akram.

"How is your Dad?" Jawad asked with a serious tone.

"Thank God, he is better now."

Aziz asked, "Rooftop okay?"

"Thanks to you Lala, hasn't leaked ever since."

Prior to the official commencement of winter with the season's first snowfall, the brothers had helped Akram layer his rooftop with a fresh coat of straw and mud. They worked from six in the morning until dusk. In those days, Akram's father had fallen ill, and was bedridden. Sharp pain had stabbed his waistline. A doctor at Kabul's Aliabad hospital had instructed him to refrain from heavy lifting until the medicine did its magic and rid his body of the needling gallstone.

Sekandar had repeatedly reminded his children that every man in Deh Darya, including Qayoum Khan, took part in building the house in which they grew up. Therefore, they can never turn their back to anyone in the village.

When the brothers discovered that Akram's father was bedridden, they didn't even wait for Akram to ask for help. One evening, after hauling rocks all day long, they knocked on Akram's door, and instructed him to prepare the straw and soil mixture, so they could get to work as soon as possible.

***

In Deh Darya and the surrounding villages, Aziz and Jawad were the only boys who had hauled rocks for a living—day after day and year after year. Joining them, some boys had tried to learn the trade. After all, there were plenty of rocks on the mountains for everyone to share. Nevertheless, no one had been able to go through the muscle ripping, bone crushing tyranny of uprooting, rolling, and hauling rocks down the mountain more than three or four consecutive days. Aziz and Jawad have been digging into the heart of Hindu Kush since their teenage years, and for that reason alone they had won every working-man's respect.

***

"Let's go inside. It's time to eat," Aziz said. Nobody argued.

Upon entering the compound, Masih heard Qayoum Khan warning Noor, "Careful *bacha*, boy. Don't let the rice get mushy." Khan had trimmed his gray beard with precision. A new sky-blue turban complemented his dark blue vest and the white traditional garment tailored by Nafas Gul. Taking brisk steps, he paced back and forth between the kitchen at a corner of the courtyard and a pair of clay fire-pits built for occasions as such on the front yard. Flames licked the inner walls of the pits and the bottom of the two massive copper cooking pots housing enough rice and beef to feed the entire village.

The waft rising from the bowls of shredded fried carrots, fried raisins, and beef stew blended with the smoke from underneath the oversized pots. The fragrance made the prospect of enjoying Noor's famous *qabeli palaw* even more real.

Noor, the tall lanky boy, whose bangs danced around his brows, poked a stick at the partially burnt oak logs, attempting to temper with the rate at which the flames were reducing them into ashes. It was about time for the rice to sit on low heat and simmer for about half hour before being served to the starving crowd. *Nawroz* or not, whenever Masih had gone to Qayoum Khan's house, he had found Noor busy either washing dishes, sweeping the courtyard, watering the vegetable garden, chopping wood, or the usual—cooking. Regardless of the task, Noor always remained focused and moved briskly.

Three years after Noor's birth, his father had gone to India on a business trip, with a plan to import textiles in return for exporting dried fruits and nuts. But upon his arrival in Delhi, he had met an irresistibly beautiful *kanchani*, a prostitute in one of the city's brothels. He had converted her to Islam, committed her to a *toba*, repentance, and then married her. Never to return, he left his wife and three-year-old son behind and settled in India.

***

With his chin down, Noor mostly stared at the ground, busy doing this or that. What was going on in his mind? Why didn't he talk much? At the time of his father's disappearance, he wasn't old enough to remember him. Maybe he was still mourning the sudden death of his mother four years after his father vanished. By then, he could clearly remember his mother. Following the loss of his parents, Noor was either serving in Qayoum Khan's house or working in his store after school. For a year though, when he dropped out of sixth grade, he sold cigarettes and chewing gums on the crowded streets of Kabul. From dawn to dusk, Noor would walk around Jada-e Maiwand, Deh Afghanan, and Shahr-e Naw, offering his merchandise to pedestrians all over the city. However, in the end, street vending did not work out for him.

One afternoon, he was beaten unconscious and robbed by a gang of three. He was beaten because he had resisted the assault, swinging the wooden box that served as his mobile store, at his attackers. Although he remembered the blinding flicker of a knife blade in the midst of the brawl, luckily he was not stabbed. However, after hurling countless kicks and punches at his face, back, and ribs, they had left him to die on the sidewalk and stolen everything he had—his entire inventory. Had a passerby not taken him to the hospital, Noor would not have been alive today.

Although his duties at Qayoum Khan's compound, and occasionally work on the mountain with Aziz and Jawad kept him busy, it never gave him any real hope for a future.

***

Despite his reserved demeanor, Noor always attempted a smile when saying hello to Masih.

"How is it going *maktabi*, schoolboy?" he looked up and squinted to prevent smoke from burning his eyes.

"All right, I guess. What's for lunch?"

"Qabeli, what else? Qabeli for Kabuli. That's all you city people eat, isn't it?" he said grinning.

"Not true. We eat all kinds of food."

"Oh yeah? Like *shir o parata*, milk and pancake for breakfast and kabob for dinner?"

"You could say that. But you are the one surrounded by cattle. You should be eating kabob all day long," Masih said smiling.

"Yeah, but they're not mine. I am a simple *dehati*, villager. My food is bread and tea, bread and onion, and if I'm lucky, bread with some yogurt. You should try them sometimes."

"Maybe I will. But right now, *qabeli* is all I'm thinking about."

As Qayoum Khan stood and watched, Noor drained the water in which the rice was boiling. A *chapan*, robe draped over the Khan's shoulders that looked almost like the one Father used to wear when he went for a walk. Having been assured that the rice would not turn soggy, Khan headed for the *burj*, the tower. Mulla Salim, Sekandar, and a few other village elders accompanied him in climbing up the forty-three step high spiraling stairway. Masih had counted them several times, and every time he had come up with the same number.

The rest of the crowd, Aziz, Jawad, Sarwar, and the rest of hisgroup members strolled behind them while the teenage boys still hung around the courtyard. As the men stepped up the stairs, the boys began to talk and laugh louder, exchanging friendly elbow and shoulder blows. Masih stood under the only tree in the courtyard that seemed to be reviving back to life after a long and harsh winter.

"Still there Kabuli?" Noor asked shooting a glance at Masih.

"I'm hungry. When is it going to be ready?"

"Patience brother, patience. When it comes to cooking, you have to take your time," Noor lifted his head up again. But this time he wasn't looking at Masih. This time, his gaze followed an attractive girl who walked past him toward the kitchen.

***

She was an inch or two taller than the other girl walking next to her. Her light skin, long dark eyelashes, and cascading black hair caught the attention of every teenage boy who stood around the compound. In addition to her stunning looks, her red shirt and the orange scarf sprinkled with tiny pink flowers also made it difficult for the boys to prevent their eyes from following her.

But Masih's gaze followed that of Noor's. As she was walking by him, in a fraction of a second, she looked up and threw a quick glance—what Afghan classical poets call *teer-e negah*, the arrow of a gaze aimed at Noor. All of this happened while she continued to walk. But wait! Was her glance accompanied by a faint smile, or did it fall on him when she just *happened* to be returning the favor? Masih's watchful eyes traveled back and forth between Noor and Sori at lightening speed. He hoped to catch her tossing one more look, just one more shot at Noor, the *Majnoon,* Romeo. One more indiscretion would convert his nagging feeling of suspicion into certainty, based on empirical evidence, that there was something seriously wrong going on between them. But, Sori held her head up and kept striding.

Yet, it wasn't too difficult for Masih to come up with an answer to his question. In fact, he had drawn his conclusion from the very moment Sori looked up and hurled that arrow at Noor. And did Noor enjoy being hit or what? Among at least a dozen boys standing in that courtyard, it was Noor, a servant, an orphan, a boy with no prospect of a bright future whatsoever, and no particular glory in his family's history, who was chosen. *Un*-believable!

Yes, Masih knew the exact meaning of that kind of exchange between a girl and a boy. He had seen Jawad trading the same kind of looks and smiles with some of the *Kochi*, nomad girls. Last summer, Jawad had taken him twice for a walk along the riverbank on the outskirts of the village. Both times, the *Kochi* ladies happened to be fetching water from the opposite banks of the river. While looking up more than once or twice, a few would smile toward Jawad who toddled on the opposite side. Sometimes, the girls flung comments at each other in Pashto, and then busted into laughter. Meanwhile, they didn't seem to notice Masih, who walked right next to Jawad—a reality he didn't necessarily like.

***

At last, Masih decided to head for the stairs leading to the *burj*, the tower. It was pointless to stand there and witness any more of that nonsense. He was not up to watching another scene from *Laili o Majnoon*, Romeo and Juliet drama upon Sori's exit from the kitchen. Without a doubt, that shameless boy had stolen her heart, and Masih could do nothing about it. But wait. Perhaps there *was* something he could do to make Noor pay for his indiscretion.

He could explain in details the entire event as he had just witnessed to Aziz and Jawad. For sure, they would teach him a lesson on how not to look with an evil eye at anyone's *namoos*, honor.

NINE

Masih sprinted up the forty-three steps and stood by the doorway to fill his lungs with fresh air rushing through the open windows. Had it not been for the entrance, which led to a small squared hallway, the shape of the tower would have been a perfect circle.

"Here," Baba invited him with the usual patting on the mattress.

Leaving his shoes among a pile of some fifty other pairs, he entered the room. Now, he had to cover a long distance before making it to the other side where Baba, Qayoum Khan, and Mulla Salim comfortably lounged against large pillows. Crossing the room seemed like a journey to eternity. He felt every single pair of eyes piercing through him just because he happened to be a boy whose father was missing. Earlier, he had noticed people staring and even pointing at him in the mosque. He had heard that petty sound people made with the tip of their tongue while looking at him, "Zchok, zchok, . . . his father . . . been a long time . . . poor boy!"

People knew Dr. Sharif well. Whenever they heard of his arrival in Deh Darya, they would flock to Baba's house and ask for a *noskha*, a prescription. A *noskha* would do the trick. For any ailment, be it a headache, or loss of eyesight, it would mean the passport to the land of wellness, especially when it was prescribed by Dr. Sharif.

Masih sat next to Baba, crossing his legs and keeping his spine straight. He remembered what Father used to say, *"Always sit straight and keep your chin up."* Yet, within seconds, he found himself pretending to examine his fingernails. The elderly man, sitting on his left, leaned toward him and said, "May God rescue your father from the hands of the infidels."

Before Masih had a chance to thank him or say something nice in return, another man added, "With the blessing of God and the power of our brave fighters, he will be free in no time, *Ensha'Allah,* God willing." With a matter of fact tone resonating in his voice, he caught the attention of a few men who sat near him. They nodded, repeating the last phrase of his sentence, *"Ensha'Allah, Ensha'Allah."*

Glancing at the far-right corner of the room, where Sarwar, Aziz, Jawad and other members of the *mujahedin* group sat in silence, Mulla Salim said, "God bless our young warriors." All eyes followed his gaze. Masih took a deep sigh, feeling the burden of attention fall off his shoulders.

Sarwar cleared his throat and tried to sound humble, "Mulla *Sayb,* Sir, with your prayers, we will succeed."

As he finished his sentence, Noor appeared in the doorway, holding a thick folded plastic mat. Younger boys, sitting next to Sarwar, began helping Noor unfold and neatly spread the mat on the floor. Long and wide, it covered almost the entire room. It was, undoubtedly, the largest eating mat anyone possessed in the village. Then, they followed Noor downstairs to deliver trays loaded with *qabeli, kabob,* steamy bowls of beef stew, salad, and of course the yogurt drink, *dogh.* Taking a few extra trips, Noor was able to bring everything upstairs by himself. Sure, he was a skinny boy, but not weak. He was the kind people referred to as *tasma,* the whip—lean and strong. The fact that he worked longer hours than anyone else around Qayoum Khan's compound and assisted Aziz and Jawad on the mountains was a testimony to his stamina and strength.

People of Deh Darya always participated in completing any project that required collaboration, be it digging a well or erecting a wall. It simply was not acceptable for one person to do the work all by himself as everyone else watched and did nothing to help. That was not the way of life in Deh Darya, and the youth who rushed to assist Noor were well aware of the rule.

Masih's age was within the helpers' age bracket. He too, should have made a trip downstairs to, at least, deliver the water pitcher. But he didn't. He was not going to help the boy who had looked at Sori in a seductive way, not a chance.

After the youngsters rushed downstairs, silence hovered in the atmosphere with the exception of a couple of whispers blending with a soft whooshing sound of a breeze that passed through. During those awkward moments, everyone waited for one of the elders to say something, anything.

Finally, Mulla Salim decided to respond to the comment that Sarwar had made prior to Noor's entry.

"*Qomandan sayb*, Sir Commander," he said to Sarwar, "may God keep you safe and bless you with health. You are the leader of our young soldiers now. You are our only hope. As long as you fight in the path of God, we are all," he swept a quick look around the room, "with you."

Qomandan sayb? Since when has Sarwar become a Sir? Masih wondered. The boy who wasted his entire life harassing people, dog fighting, and smoking hashish, that boy is now a commander *and* a respected one. How could Mulla Salim bring himself to call him that? Doesn't he know who Sarwar really is? What a shame!

Qayoum Khan jumped in, knowing that his son would not be able to offer an eloquent response, "Mulla Sayb, I am confident that with the blessing of your prayers and the support of boys like Sekandar's sons, God willing they will be triumphant."

The elderly man who sat next to Masih, the one who had started the whole conversation, shifted his weight from one hip to the other and said, "Sekandar's sons have been there for the village in good times and in bad. They can topple an entire mountain. Not many men have the same kind of *ghairat*, honor that they do."

Except for Sekandar himself, who responded with a faint smile while beaming with pride, everyone nodded in affirmation. Aziz and Jawad kept their gazes fixed on the plastic mat.

Sekandar straightened his slightly hunched back, and said loud enough so everybody could hear, "My sons will never be able to pay their dues to all of you. We will always be in debt to you and especially to Qayoum Khan."

The boys' footsteps could be heard climbing up the stairs. Moments later, they entered the room carrying extra-large copper trays filled to the brim with rice and topped with kabob. Two of the teens who entered last, were delivering some three dozen long loafs of steaming *naan*, bread. The aroma of blended dishes replaced the muddled tang of Pakistani perfumes that had drifted from the mosque all the way up to the tower. Seconds later, Noor entered the room, balancing a large crystal bowl of *dogh*, the yogurt drink between his hands.

"Good job son, you made it on time," Qayoum Khan said.

"The women helped," Noor bent to place the bowl in front of Khan, his hair swinging over his wet forehead.

The women? Who exactly helped? Was Sori one of them? Unbelievable. Actually, it shouldn't be all that surprising that something was going on between Noor and Sori. After all, they were classmates from first to third grade. Plus, some days when Noor, Jawad, and Aziz finished their work on the mountain, the brothers would take Noor home to have dinner with them. Noor and Sori's brothers were friends. How could he do such a thing? How could he be friends with her brothers, go inside their house, eat their *naan-o namak*, bread and salt, and betray their trust by seducing their sister? No doubt, he was a good example of what Father would have called a *bai-ghairat*, a dishonorable man.

Maybe it would not be a bad idea to, somehow, let Aziz or Jawad know what this seemingly poor and innocent boy was up to. If the secret was revealed, the brothers wouldn't just end their friendship with him; they wouldn't even let him get away with a *gosh-mali*, ear rubbing. They would take him up on the mountain and push him off a cliff, so the wolves could enjoy a free lunch.

Although Noor's bones would definitely deserve to be, in Father's words, softened a little, pushing him off a cliff seemed a bit too harsh a punishment. *I'll have to think about this,* Masih said to himself.

While he wouldn't mind eating a little, he would not take as much as a sip from that *dogh*, yogurt drink that Noor had prepared. Instead, he will drink water. A fire blazed inside him.

TEN

It could have been heavy rain spattering against the window, or perhaps the discovery of the relationship between Sori and Noor that kept Masih awake for a good part of the night. But eventually, he did fall asleep.

In the morning, facing the assaulting rays of the sun from behind the window, he opened his eyes. It must have been around nine or even ten o'clock. Way too late for Masih to wake up. The clouds had melted away, allowing the sun to lift an intense aroma of the damp soil around the village.

Ignoring the fresh morning breeze, he pulled the comforter over his head to catch a few more precious minutes of sleep. Seconds later, the jingle of Sori's bangles caressed his ears. With his eyes still shut, he visualized shiny red, orange, purple, yellow, white, and pink circles glittering in the sun—a picture in motion that was not a dream. It was better.

"Masih . . ."

He opened his eyes, pushing the comforter away and found Sori standing next to him.

"Come on, get up. I'll warm up some milk for you," she said with a sweet, gentle tone.

As Masih enjoyed a fried egg, Baba said, "Eat son, eat. You have a long journey ahead." He sat on the mattress across from him, twirling a string of shiny-green prayer beads.

"Where are the boys, Baba?" Masih asked, sipping tea.

"Up on the mountain. It's messy up there, but they could still get some work done," Baba sensed Masih's concern that he would not be able to say goodbye to them before leaving for the city. "Don't worry; they will be back before you finish your breakfast."

"They will come. Let's get ready. We don't want to miss the bus," Mother said, tying the corners of a gray scarf under her chin.

A few minutes later, Masih slipped into his worn-out jeans and a T-shirt, on the front of which Bruce Lee seemed prepared to deliver a serious blow to his opponent. Nadia exited the room and sat next to the bare rosebushes. Contemplating, she looked at her watch a couple of times. Masih realized that Mother didn't want to talk to Baba Sekandar, who was sitting inside. Maybe she wanted to listen to the sound of the rushing water on the other side of the wall, or maybe she just preferred to be alone as she often did after Father's disappearance.

With a final glance at her watch, she stood up, turned around and called, "Let's go, Masih. Zaman is not going to wait for us forever." On the way back to Kabul, Zaman's bus passed by Deh Darya between the hours of ten and ten-thirty. The next bus would not show up until around noon.

Masih wished he could tell his mother that he didn't want to go back. Watching Aziz, Jawad, and other boys in Deh Darya strengthened his patriotic feelings. If they could fight for Afghanistan, he could fight too. He wanted to fulfil his *farz*, religious duty by taking part in the fight against the people who had taken away his father. When the Soviets left and when the government was toppled, Father will return home. Why not, then, expedite the process so he could come home sooner? Plus, what else could be cooler than being armed, and walking up and down the mountains surrounding the village? What would be more exciting than planning and executing the next attack on the Soviets? Aziz had said that the rocket launchers would soon arrive from Pakistan. And, Masih knew a thing or two about the mountains.

Up there, the sun shined brighter and the wind blew a lot stronger than anywhere in the world. He remembered, up there seeing nothing but bulging rocks of a thousand shapes and sizes, which seemed like mountains unto themselves. Smaller bits were just perfect for a rock-throwing contest or ammo for a slingshot, like the one that Aziz used to carry around before getting a hold of the Kalashnikov.

Masih had seen the eagle, the partridge, and the hawk either sitting on a rock or flying around the deep valleys and ravines. He had heard their cries bouncing off the boulders and vanishing into the sky. From up there, Masih had also seen the river. Filled with liquid silver, it carved its way through the village, the valleys, and the farmlands, eventually joining the Kabul River, which cut through the city.

But no, it was impossible for him to stay in the village. Mother wouldn't agree to that, and Masih could not leave her all alone in the city. *Take care of your mother. Always obey her, and finish school.* Father's last words resonated in his mind. How could he disobey his father *and* his mother? He finished his tea and stood up to prepare for his trip back to Kabul.

***

"God, please rescue my father," Masih murmured while standing on the side of the road next to Nadia. Sekandar and Sori had also raised their hands in prayer. They prayed for Mahro and all others resting in the cemetery. The practice had become a tradition as the family entered and also when left the village for as long as he could remember.

***

Standing on the roadside, they stared at the desolate street meandering through the mountains from *Deh Bala*, the Upper Village, all the way to Kabul.

"I hope Zaman's bus broke down again so you can stay one more night with us," Sori smiled.

No one offered an answer. Masih kept looking at the road. Apparently, Nadia and Sekandar didn't have much to say to each other either. That seemed strange.

A few minutes later, Masih saw the shimmering reflection of the sun bouncing off the windshield of Zaman's vehicle. He squinted at the dusty road across and saw no signs of Aziz and Jawad approaching. Maybe it wasn't in his *nasib*, destiny to say goodbye to his friends. He looked toward the arriving vehicle and glanced at the dusty road again. This time, he saw the brothers marching toward the main street. Something dangled off Jawad's fingertips that Masih couldn't identify clearly. A box? Maybe a cage?

"Sorry sister, we got trapped. There was mud everywhere; it is a lot worse than we thought," Aziz said, pointing at his own spattered clothes.

"It's okay. I'm glad you made it. Masih would have been disappointed to have left without saying goodbye to you."

"We would never let him go home like that," Aziz said, raising a hand behind Masih's neck.

Realizing that the spade was about to land on his back, he stood firm to prevent his face from hitting the ground.

Then, Jawad offered the cage to him, "It's yours, with your mother's permission of course."

The cage was painted metallic gold. In it, the Paper Whites sat quietly, not paying much attention to the outside world. Masih looked at Mother.

Nadia said, "That's nice, but Jawad, what is he going to do with this? He is going to be busy with schoolwork, and I won't be able to climb up the rooftops after him."

"Masih is not going to climb up the rooftops, sister." Jawad said. Then he turned to Masih, "Are you?"

"No, I won't. I *won't*," he said shaking his head.

"Can you promise?" Sekandar asked, offering a handshake.

Masih raised his hand without hesitation, looked the old man in the eye and shook, "I promise."

Hearing the assured voice of her son and witnessing the firm handshake brought a smile to Nadia's face. Her boy was becoming a man.

"You have to promise to take good care of them too," she said.

"Promise Mother; I promise."

Aziz bent down, held Masih's arms with a powerful, yet gentle grip, "We're not giving them to you so you climb up the rooftops. Take care of them for a while, then, when the time is right, let them go. They don't belong to this cage or a dove-house. They must have come from *Sakhi jan*." He was referring to one of the city's popular shrines. "If you let them free, they will find their way back to where they belong. One day, we will set our flock free too. That's my promise to you."

Jawad was still holding the cage. Masih looked at it and then turned his pleading eyes to Mother.

She drew a deep breath, "Take it, but remember; you will have to study *and* take care of them."

Changing hands, the cage swung. The doves stood up, seemingly concerned and even frightened, as if they knew that a change was occurring in their life.

"Don't let them go hungry. You'll have to answer to God if you do," Aziz reached into one of his vest pockets, drew a bag of birdfeed, and handed it to Masih.

The bus had been idling for at least five minutes. Khalifa Zaman had placed it in neutral and patiently stared at the road extending to Kabul. Every few seconds, he took a puff off the cigarette in his right hand, as his other hand rested on the steering wheel.

When saying goodbye, Sori repeated the annoying habit of holding Masih's chin and planting the *pachchi*, smooch on his cheek.

Mother and Baba's farewell was shorter and more formal than any other time.

***

When Masih climbed into the bus, Khalifa asked, nodding toward the cage, "Since when have you become a *kafter-baz*, pigeon keeper?"

Before Masih had an opportunity to answer, Nadia said, "He already was one; he just didn't have the pigeons."

"Remember, I am charging double for them," Zaman smiled, then placed the vehicle in first gear and softly let his feet off the clutch. She began moving with the usual roar, leaving a dark cloud of fuming smoke behind. The guests waved goodbye to their hosts still standing on the roadside.

Masih put the cage down in between his feet. He imagined the envious look on the faces of the neighborhood boys seeing his birds for the first time. *Cool!* He said to himself.

Terrified, the pigeons moved their heads from side to side, trying to find out what was happening. *Why is this noisy box rattling? What happened to the other doves?* They probably wanted to ask. If Masih pretended to speak to them, telling them that everything will be all right, other passengers would think he had lost his mind. He kept quiet. Thank God, birds don't know humans' language. If they did, they would have demanded an explanation for their situation.

I'm keeping you in jail, so I can feel good. It doesn't matter if it makes you sad or frightened. What matters is that you keep me company. He looked up, trying not to think.

Then, he caught a side view of Mother's profile. Her eyes remained fixed on the slopes of the distant mountains and the farmland that seemed to be moving backward as the bus pushed ahead. Maybe she needed some time to herself. Occasionally, a person just needs a little privacy.

Since the night the Secret Police had taken Father away, Masih too often found himself not wanting to talk to anyone, including Mother. At times, he wouldn't want to do anything, not even play soccer or create any new designs. He just wanted to hide in his room, away from the world—the world that had stolen his father.

Once in solitude, he would think about everything he and Father did together. In his mind, they would walk to Baharestan cinema to watch an Indian movie, enjoy an ice cream, and buy a steaming plate of chickpeas from a street vendor. Father loved to go for walks, and he did so at least three times a week. Sometimes, Masih would keep him company. He used to say, "Walking prevents all kinds of illnesses." Then he would smile and add, "Kieep it a secret between us. If everybody finds out, I'll go out of business." Masih would smile back, but Father would want to hear a laughter. Therefore, he would resort to tickling the back of his neck, "I just said something very funny and didn't hear a good laugh."

Masih would burst into laughter while trying to slip out of his scrawny grip.

What would it be like when Father returns home? What would that day look like? Would it be a sunny day or a rainy one? What time of the day would Father arrive? Often, Masih would close his eyes, and play and replay in his mind the imaginary scene in which Father surprised him with his return. That moment will finally come. *One day, I will see Father again.*

***

As one of the tires fell into a pothole, a strong tremor broke his train of thoughts. "Mother, what's going on? You look sad."

"Nothing. I am just tired."

"Are you sure? Why don't you tell me what's wrong?"

66

"What do you want me to say?"

"I don't know; whatever is on your mind. You always tell me not to hide anything from you. Now I think you're hiding something from me."

"You shouldn't worry about adults' business."

"Mother, I'm not a child any more."

The bus came to a stop. One person stepped out while about a dozen new passengers boarded. A commotion began, but Masih and Mother remained quiet as he waited for her to say something.

Still staring out the window, Mother finally broke the silence, "Baba is marrying Sori to Sarwar."

She must have said something else, Masih thought. That can't be true. How could Baba do such a thing?

"What?" he had to confirm, "to Qayoum Khan's son?"

"Yes. That's what he's going to do."

"Who told you?"

"Baba, himself."

"Does Sori know about this?"

"She has no idea. Baba doesn't know how to tell her. He is waiting for Nawroz to pass. Then, he will break the news to her."

"Sori hates that guy. She will never marry him," Masih said, remembering his conversation with her just two days ago.

"I know. Sori is a gem, and Sarwar is . . . How *stupid!* But it's not up to her."

Masih could not think of any reason for Baba's decision. Why would Baba agree to wed his daughter to a boy who had no education and no manners? Sarwar smokes hashish, gambles all the time, and is a *chaqo-kaash*, knife fighter. He does nothing to help anybody. He is nothing like his father.

"Mother, you have to stop him."

"I can't. I spent hours arguing with him," she sighed, "it was useless. My word has no value to him. *His chicken has only one leg*," she said, meaning Baba was a stubborn man.

Masih visualized Sori in a green traditional wedding gown and Sarwar standing next to her with a dull expression on his face. Then, he imagined Sori and Noor as bride and groom, both are all smiles— a much better-suited couple. At least Noor was a hard-working man, polite, humble, and an excellent chef. Although in serious need of a haircut, he wasn't a bad looking boy either. Sori and Noor would make a nice pair and could definitely have beautiful children. Noor always spoke few words, while Sori had an opinion about everything. That could have worked perfectly well for them. She would have done all the talking, and he would have listened all the time.

"But it doesn't make sense, Mother. Why is Baba doing this?"

"He says that he has to, because it's the honorable thing to do."

"I don't understand. What's so honorable about marrying your daughter to a loser?"

"It's a long, complicated story."

"It's not that she just doesn't like Sarwar. She hates him."

Khalifa Zaman's bus began to get crowded as he made two more stops and picked up more passengers. Apparently, everybody was heading for Kabul. Thank God, it wasn't one of those summer days where the hot-dusted air became stifling when it mixed with the stench of sweat and a diverse assortment of cheap perfumes inside the crowded bus. It was just another clear spring day where life resurged as the sun awakened the earth from hibernation.

"There is nothing Sori can do. She can disagree with Baba, but that doesn't change anything. I know her father. Whatever *he* decides is going to happen, that's it. Sekandar won't listen to anybody."

"Sori says Sarwar was the one who torched the school. She already hates him for ruining her dreams." *She likes someone else.* Masih was tempted to tell Mother all about what had happened between Sori and Noor. But no, that would not be wise. During a heated discussion between Mother and Baba about Sori's fate, if the information jumped out of Mother's mouth, Noor and Sori will be in serious trouble. Who knows? Maybe once Sori finds out about her father's decision, she elopes with Noor. But, if their secret were out, running away is not going to be an option.

Nadia said, "I don't blame her. But she has no choice. Baba will sacrifice anything to prove his loyalty to Qayoum Khan."

"Aziz and Jawad aren't friends with Sarwar. How come they are in his group?"

"They have to follow him."

"No they don't, they could join a different group," Masih said.

"I know; they never got along with him. A couple of times they even got into fights when they were teenagers. You were too little to remember."

"Then why did they join his group?"

"Quiet!" Mother whispered, "You are talking too loud. I told you they had to. Everything is in Sarwar's hands. Stop it now."

She was concerned that a *mokhber,* an informant from KhAD might be in the crowded vehicle—the kind of *mokhber* who had falsely accused her husband of having ties with the anti-government forces.

Masih looked down to check on his doves. Accustomed to the constant jolts and jerks of the bus ride by now, they seemed relaxed. He had not seen anybody in the neighborhood who owned a pair of doves as beautiful as that. Masih thought about what Aziz had said. They didn't look like just any doves. They must have belonged to a shrine. He would keep them in his own room, so they won't freeze during those chilly spring nights.

***

The bus passed by Qala-e Naw and kept pushing to reach Bala Tapa. This meant that they were only half an hour away from Kabul. The dirt road in Bala Tapa transformed into a paved and wide street. A velvety green hill decorated with rocks, boulders, and trees stood behind the stores that lined up on both sides of the road. People of Bala Tapa had built their clay-houses over those hills. Only a handful were assembled with bricks and mortar.

To pass through the bazaar, Khalifa Zaman brought the vehicle's speed to about fifteen miles per hour. He had to share the road with street vendors, donkey-drawn carriages, bicycles, motorcycles, and taxicabs.

Nadia opened her briefcase and fished out two spicy *bolanis,* fried dumplings stuffed with leek and mashed potato, which Sori had prepared in the morning. Usually, Masih would gobble four or five of those within minutes. Today, however, he had lost his appetite. He only had one. Lost in thoughts, Nadia could barely finish hers.

As Nadia closed the bag, with a sudden violent jolt her forehead banged against the handrail in front of her seat. Khalifa had slammed on the brake. She looked at her son to make sure he was unharmed. Thank God, Masih had clenched a pole next to him just in time. In a frenzy, passengers had reached for any part of the vehicle they could grab. The terrified doves fluttered their wings, trying to escape. Shocked passengers shot frantic glances at each other and through the windshield, attempting to understand what had caused the sudden blow.

"Mother, you okay?"

"I am fine son. Don't worry," she said as a sore spot began to surface on her forehead.

Nobody had felt an impact or heard a collision. Even though it seemed not to be an accident, Nadia's heart sank as she looked outside.

ELEVEN

Across the street, a military truck was parked along the sidewalk. Two soldiers stood guard behind it. Something worth protection must have been hidden inside. Without a doubt, the vehicle belonged to *qowwa-e talashi*, the Army's recruiting division that terrified any mother raising a teenage son. Its mission: kidnap any young boy who seems old enough to sling a Kalashnikov over his shoulder. Technically, if a boy could prove that he was eighteen or younger, or was a student, *and* if he didn't get into an argument with the recruiting officer questioning the validity of his I.D., he would remain exempt from service. Otherwise, within a couple of weeks he would find himself in the battlefield.

Nadia scrambled in her handbag with trembling fingers to find Masih's student identification card. Fumbling a few times, she finally pulled out the document.

"Here, hold on to it," her voice quivered.

Although, Masih was legally too young to be considered for conscription, Nadia knew that the law did not necessarily guarantee the safety of her son. At Balkhi elementary school, where she taught the third graders, her colleagues had told numerous horror stories about how the Army's *qowwa-e talashi* had abducted boys as young as thirteen-years-old from the streets of Kabul, many of whom were never to be found. The story of Fatima's brother, Reza, was one of the exceptional few without a tragic ending.

***

Following Mother's gaze, Masih too noticed the military vehicle parked across the street. The machineguns that slung over the soldiers' shoulders seemed identical to the ones that Aziz and Jawad were carrying. Through the windshield, he could see a man in military uniform standing in the middle of the road. With a stern expression on his face, he had kept the palm of his hand raised toward the vehicle to make sure it stopped and remained as such.

Moments later, a soldier climbed into the vehicle. The stomping of his boots echoed amidst the utter silence in the bus.

"Where are you heading Khalifa?" he didn't bother to greet.

"Kabul," Zaman's serious tone almost matched that of the soldier's. Masih, however, sensed a slight quiver in his voice unnoticeable to an unfamiliar ear.

The young officer, who seemed only four or five years older than Masih, shook his head with a simple "*Kho*, okay."

Then he faced the passengers, and with a piercing stare began to scan around the bus in slow motion. His dark, tired eyes moved from side to side, like a pair of swinging pendulums. His face, with cheekbones protruding from behind his tanned skin reminded Masih of the skeleton standing on a corner of the biology lab in school.

In an effort to avoid appearing nervous, everyone, including Masih, looked up, staring him back in the eye. He was in the hunt for somebody, perhaps a young boy who didn't attend school and wasted his time loitering around girls' high schools—a recruit. Certainly, Masih's description did not match the criteria. For this soldier, finding that kind of a boy would mean faster discharge from the service, which would help him avoid facing the *mujahedin*, the likes of Aziz and Jawad on the battleground.

While the terrified passengers waited to hear him make some sort of an announcement, the soldier bit his upper lip, contemplating for a few seconds. He had nothing to say. What's there to say? He couldn't find what he was looking for, so better move on to the next bus.

Straightening his weapon's strap on his shoulder, he turned around and began to step down. Then, as his left foot touched the ground, he paused and climbed back into the bus, as if he was struck by an idea.

"You," he said pointing his index finger at the old man sitting behind Masih.

The man didn't respond.

"Hey boy! I am talking to you. Stand up," he shouted with an irritated tone. This time, he made it clear that he wasn't talking to the old man. He was barking orders at Masih.

"Who, me?" Masih asked pointing at his own chest and immediately feeling embarrassed about his failed attempt at claiming ignorance.

"Of course you," the officer answered with a rude, condescending tone. "Do you have your I.D. on you?"

"Yes."

"Bring it."

With a doubtful glance at Mother, he stood up. Nadia's face turned as white as the color of the doves sitting next to her feet. As Masih began to take a step, she grabbed his left arm, "*Bishi!* Sit down," she ordered loud and clear, so the soldier could hear. Passengers' weary eyes swung back and forth between the soldier, who was clearly fuming, and the mother and son, who were visibly frightened.

"*Amr ast*, It's an order. Get out," the soldier shouted again, pointing his index finger toward the sidewalk.

"My son is a student. He's only fifteen-years-old," Nadia said, trying to maintain her composure.

"He has to prove it."

They locked eyes, like boxers moments prior to throwing the first punch.

"Let's go son," she said to Masih.

The officer descended. Nadia and Masih followed him to the sidewalk.

"Give me your student I.D.," he demanded, raising the palm of his right hand.

"Here," Masih offered the card. It was spotless, without a crease or even a blemish. Unlike many other boys, who kept their I.D. in the back pocket of their jeans, Masih saved his in the upper pocket of his shirt. Therefore, his I.D. remained in mint condition.

The man pushed the rim of his hat up and fixed his eyes on the document. He flipped it, furrowing his sharp eyebrows, and turned it over again. Then he held it close to his face, as if he had trouble reading.

"What's your name?" he asked without looking up.

"Masih Ahmad Sharif."

"Father's name?"

"Asad Ahmad Sharif."

"Grade?"

"This year, I'm starting tenth grade," he swiftly answered as Mother stood next to him.

"But here it says you are in ninth grade," the officer said lifting an eyebrow.

Nadia jumped in, "That's—"

Wanting to handle the situation himself, Masih didn't let her finish, "That's from last year, when I was in ninth grade."

"I know how to count. You don't have to explain," he looked up, sounding annoyed, "the only problem is," he paused to dramatize the situation.

"What is the problem?" Nadia asked, "What's wrong?"

The officer tapped the card with the back of his left hand, "You say your name is Masih Ahmad, while here it says Ahmad Masih, *and* I don't see any last name on this. There is no Sharif here."

"The clerk has made a mistake—"

This time Nadia took charge, "What's the difference? My son's name is Masih and his father is Asad. It says so right there," she pointed at the I.D. in the soldier's clutch.

"No, it doesn't. You think I am stupid?"

"*Bachem*, son I swear to God, this *is* his card."

"How is it possible when someone else's name is on it?" He frowned. Then, staring Masih in the eye, he held the paper up and began ripping it into pieces. After tearing the card in half, he neatly placed the pieces on top of each other and tore them again. He then put the shreds in his baggy trousers' pocket.

"Take him," he called on one of the soldiers who stood waiting across the street.

"Take him?" Nadia asked in protest, "Where? Why?"

"*Hamshira*, sister, I explained to you once. I can't explain again," he began to walk away.

"Hey! You didn't explain anything. My son has a valid I.D. Why did you rip it? What kind of a human, what kind of a Muslim are you?" she followed him.

"Quiet! It's not appropriate for a woman your age to raise her voice like this. Go. Stop harassing me," he said through his clenched teeth.

"I am not going anywhere, and I am not going to be quiet. You destroy my son's I.D., kidnap him in front of my eyes, and tell me to be quiet? I will follow you to the end of the world."

A few pedestrians stopped and watched as she protested.

"Woman, don't make a scene. It's better for your son to take up arms and defend the *namoos*, the honor of his country instead of wasting his time on the streets."

"*I* am his *namoos*. He is taking care of me. He is the only son, the only child I have," Nadia said. Then, she softened her tone, "Have mercy *Zabet Sayb*, officer. You will see *sawab*, reward in return. He is like your little brother, too young for military service."

"Aren't *I* too young to be a soldier? If I can defend my country against the Pakistanis and the Americans, why can't he? Is his blood thicker than mine?" Veins popped on his forehead, as his voice ascended progressively with every word..

"May God protect you and all other young men like you. May no mother's heart be injured with the loss of her son," tears rolled down Nadia's face.

"Your prayer is not going to help me. If you care about this country, then let your son fulfill his duty."

"But my son is just a baby. I beg you. For God's sake, look at him. He is too young to carry a gun," she said, unsuccessfully trying to reach for Masih's arm as he began to step away.

Masih didn't want to cross the street with the soldier. But he didn't want to be dragged to the truck either, so he kept walking.

Watching him climb into the back of the military vehicle, Zaman reached for the ignition, killed the engine, and squeezed his protruding belly from behind the steering wheel. He then hopped out of the bus, skipping the last step. Khalifa's helper and eleven-year-old son, Hakim followed his father with fistfuls of coins jiggling in his pockets. Rushing toward the soldier, Zaman turned and yelled at him, "Go back. Stay there and wait for me. Understand?" Sounding furious, he pointed his index finger toward the bus.

Astonished, Hakim stopped and obeyed his father's command. He couldn't quite understand why his father seemed so angry.

Masih's eyes took about a minute to adjust to the dim light in the back of the truck. The stench of diesel and dust assaulted his nostrils. With his legs crossed, he sat on the ice-cold metal across two other kidnapped boys. Frightened and silent, their eyes rapidly blinked and remained fixed on the floor.

Mother is alone, all by herself. What is she going to do? What will happen to her? As he worried, the thoughts kept swirling in his head. How will she carry groceries all the way home from Mandawi Bazaar? What if she gets sick? How would she go to the doctor's office? Without her husband and son, the house will feel like a prison. Day after day, Mother would be watching the door, waiting for the men she loves to knock. Masih couldn't help but picture her sitting in the living room, silently crying and praying for her son and husband's return.

Visualizing how difficult it would be for Mother to live the rest of her life alone, he made a promise to himself. *If I make it out of here, I would never leave her alone.*

If he were killed on the battlefield, Mother would be alone until Father's return. It is also possible that Father would never come home. The communists might take his life at any moment. At school, through the whispers and mumbles that went on among his classmates, Masih had heard heart-wrenching conclusions to stories similar to that of his father's.

O almighty God, keep him safe and bring him home. Masih prayed in silence, assured that God had heard him.

He took a deep breath and glanced around. Narrow rays of light worked their way through the tiny holes around the tarp. *So, this is how it feels to be a prisoner*, he said to himself, thinking about his pigeons.

Then, he thought about jumping out of the truck, in the same way the heroes of Indian movies did. But, this was no Indian movie, and those Kalashnikov bullets were real and could kill. He would be shot before his feet even touched the ground.

Yet, another thought entered his mind. Fighting against the *mujahedin*, he would eventually be doomed to a dishonorable death anyway. Then it is probably better to be killed sooner, since he would have to side with the same cowards who had sold out Afghanistan to the Soviets and locked up Father. So why not take the leap right now and die with dignity? If he went to *jabha*, the frontline, he would have no choice but to aim and shoot at the enemy. And who was the enemy? An Afghan who defended his country and risked his life to rescue men like Father from the bloody claws of the government.

The thought of pulling the trigger at someone like Jawad or Aziz churned Masih's stomach. If he joined the military, he could end up murdering his own brothers in order to save his own life. Subsequently, he would burn in hell for eternity, for there was no forgiveness for the despicable act of murdering one's own Muslim brother. And if he died fighting on the Soviets' side, he would still burn in hell. Mulla Salim himself had announced that whoever fights and dies in the battle against the *mujahedin*, without a doubt becomes a *mordar*, a filthy carcass. That person will never see the light of heaven. Too bad, not only Masih failed to achieve martyrdom, he was now going to die as a dishonorable coward.

Maybe his own prisoners, the white doves put a spell on him. *I hope they aren't stolen. They will at least give Mother some company.* Feeling helpless and exhausted, Masih leaned back against the metal sidewall.

***

Gleaming rivers of tears streamed from Nadia's eyes. Her headscarf had slipped over her shoulders. As she saw Zaman approaching, she raised her hands and cried, "Khalifa, what am I going to do? They took him from me in broad daylight. I want my son back. I am not going anywhere without him."

"What does he want?" he asked as he walked toward her. They had already moved Masih to the back of the truck. Was it too late?

"I told him my son is just a baby, but he didn't believe me. He ripped Masih's I.D. It's in his pocket. Do something, Khalifa. Please, do something," she said, clawing her temples.

"Officer, that boy is her only child," Khalifa approached him with a calm, respectful tone, "come on, let the kid go. You will earn *sawab*, reward in the afterworld."

"I don't need *sawab*," he said without looking at Khalifa. If I let him go, who is going to serve? Who will defend this country? Will you enlist instead of him?"

Zaman tried not to grind his teeth, "He is a too young, and I am an old man. Only brave and strong men like you can fight in a war."

The soldier turned, glancing at him eschewed, "Go uncle, don't butter me up. He is a grown-up, and you could fight if you really wanted to. On the *ashrar's*, thug's side seventy-year-olds fight."

Calling *mujahedin* thugs confirmed Khalifa's suspicion that he wasn't just any soldier. He was a pro-communist soldier, a comrade, and perhaps a member of the People's Democratic Party of Afghanistan (PDPA).

"Please, let him go," he pleaded, "God will give to you in return." If he believed in God, why would he be kidnapping a fifteen-year-old in the first place? Khalifa thought to himself as those words came out of his mouth.

The officer dipped his right hand inside the pocket of his khakis, and fished out a round metal box, small enough to fit in his palm. Then, he twisted open the top, poured a pinch of the powdered chewing tobacco into his left palm, and hurled it into his mouth.

"Look, I am just a poor soldier doing my job. I'm so poor; I can't even afford a pack of smokes. I am chewing tobacco instead. I don't know when your God is going to notice me. Go away uncle. Your prayers don't solve my problems," he slurred.

Contemplating, Khalifa Zaman paused. It took him a few seconds to process what the young soldier was telling him.

"A man like you deserves the best," he said shooting quick glances to his left and right, "I have plenty of cigarettes." Then, he looked back. Hakim was leaning against the vehicle's bumper, warily watching his father.

"Hakim, come here," Zaman shouted.

As if Hakim heard the sound of a gunshot at the start of a race, he sprinted toward him as he held on to his shirt's jiggling side-pocket that bulged with coins.

Khalifa pulled Hakim by the arm and whispered in his ear, trying to minimize the movement of his lips and facial expression, "How much cash, how much is in your pocket?"

Pedestrians shot glances at them, unable to conceal their curiosity. But, no one dared to stare or stop and ask a question.

Hakim reached into his vest's inner pocket and dug out a fistful of ten and twenty Afghani bills, "This is all I have, and lots of coins," he said with an apologetic tone.

Khalifa snatched the crumpled batch from his son's extended hand. He clumsily straightened the Afghani bills one by one.

"Sixty-five? This is not enough," he said, looking at Hakim's baffled face. Then he turned toward the soldier, who seemed to be staring at the rolling hills surrounding the market, "Give me a minute. I'll be back."

He acknowledged him with a look from the corner of his eyes without saying a word.

Khalifa marched toward his vehicle. With each hasty step, his nostrils whistled, and beneath his powder-blue, grease-stained shirt his belly wiggled. He hopped on the bus and pulled a bunch of keys out of the side pocket of his vest, with which he unlocked the glove box. Then, he produced a pack of already opened cigarettes, from which two sticks were missing. He also extracted a bundle of ten, twenty, and fifty Afghani bills, rolled and held together with a rubber band. Turning his back toward the passengers, Zaman counted a total amount of four-hundred Afghani, not including the money his son had handed him earlier. He stuffed the bundle along with the pack of cigarettes into his side pocket and leaped out of the vehicle.

**

Khalifa Zaman nervously looked across the street. Nadia was standing on the sidewalk near the truck. While the soldiers were guarding it, she was watching the soldiers, as if somehow she could stop the abduction already in progress.

When Khalifa neared, the soldier smiled, "You again?" he sounded surprised, as if he wasn't expecting him to return.

Khalifa kept strolling toward him, until there remained a couple of inches between the tips of their noses, "I won't go anywhere without taking care of you." Then, keeping his eyes fixed on the officer's leather-skinned face, he reached into his side pocket and withdrew the cash stashed along with the cigarette-pack.

"This should last you a few days," he added keeping his hand down.

"I don't burn the cheap stuff," the officer spat the chewing tobacco while stealing a glance at the content of Zaman's clenched fist.

"Me neither," he raised the pack of American Marlboro up close to his face.

The officer's lips curled into a smile. Khalifa pulled a stick from the red and white case, offering it to the soldier. Then, he produced a lighter and helped him light up the cigarette in between his thin, withered lips. The soldier closed his eyes and inhaled deep. He had not had a cigarette for a while, and not because he was concerned about his health.

"That woman has lost her husband, and now she is about to lose her only child too. But I'm not going to let that happen. I have more of these stacked at home. When you see me again on this route, all you have to do is ask."

The soldier reached for the content of Khalifa's fist. But Zaman pulled back. "The boy is *my* passenger, and he is not leaving without his I.D."

"No problem," he said, reaching into his khakis' pocket for the shredded document. As he exchanged it for the content of the driver's fist, his dexterity made Zaman wonder if he had struck such deals in the past. Then, with a loud whistle, the officer caught the attention of the guards across the street, "Let the kid go."

One of the soldiers peeked inside the back of the truck and said something. About three seconds later, Masih jumped out of the vehicle, landing firmly on both feet. Nadia hugged and showered her son with kisses and tears. Witnessing their reunion, a wide grin flashed on Khalifa Zaman's face.

The guards stood still, keeping their eyes fixed on the sidewalk. They had just lost a potential recruit, one-third of their captives for the day. And the likelihood of their comrade sharing his spoils seemed low.

During those few minutes, the passengers on the bus had witnessed a tragic story begin, unfold, and conclude with a happy ending. Shocked and yet ecstatic, Masih tried, but could not hold back his tears. So he rested his forehead on his mother's shoulder and cried.

With glazed eyes, Zaman turned to the soldeir and said, "May God bless you in return."

"I guess He already has," he said, examining the dying cigarette in between his fingers.

***

"God bless you Khalifa," Nadia said wiping tears off her face. "You have always been there for us."

Zaman handed her Masih's ripped I.D., "Please sister, don't mention it. This is nothing compared to what Dr. Sharif did for my son."

***

Four years ago, Dr. Sharif had saved Hakim's life by rescuing him from the grips of Malaria. For weeks, the doctor had made regular visits, at least twice a week to Khalifa's house. He had kept the boy under close watch, monitoring his diet and medication intake. In return, Zaman and his wife offered heartfelt thanks and prayers for his health and happiness. On many occasions, Zaman had tried to give him a payment, but the doctor had refused to accept it. He knew that if he took the payment, the next day the family would have less to eat. His goal was to see Hakim back on his feet and his parents happy. The doctor himself had a son, and couldn't imagine bearing the pain of losing him.

Eventually, he did achieve that goal, and from then on, Khalifa Zaman and his wife remained eternally grateful to him. Although Zaman would never be able to match what Dr. Sharif had done for his son, he was watchful for a chance to convey his gratitude to him.

Just a few minutes ago, he had taken advantage of such opportunity.

***

When Masih and Nadia climbed into the bus, the passengers began to whisper among themselves. Almost everyone had a comment to share.

As Nadia was taking her seat, an elderly woman leaned forward from the seat across the aisle, "You are a brave woman. I prayed for you the whole time."

Nadia forced a smile, her eyes still bloodshot, "Very kind of you. He is my only child. We need your prayers."

As soon as Khalifa brought the engine back to life, he opened the glove box and reached for another pack of cigarettes. He lit a smoke with the same lighter that he had used minutes ago, drew a long pull and exhaled, "Sorry Doc. I really need this one."

***

Masih looked out the window toward the military truck, still parked across the street with the other boys inside. He thought about them and hoped they will find a way out too. It seemed like a miracle to him that he had jumped out of that vehicle without being shot. Had Khalifa not rescued him, within a few days, he could have found himself fighting against the *mujahedin* and facing a dishonorable death. What a nightmare! His I.D. was torn, but that wasn't so bad.

Tomorrow, first thing in the morning, he would quickly get himself a new card issued—a corrected one. Then, he would laminate it, so nobody could rip it again.

TWELVE

Someone was impatiently pounding on the gate. Sekandar ended his evening prayer and sprang onto his feet. He listened again, and sure enough, the banging of the knocker continued.

"God have mercy," he muttered to himself. Before he had a chance to exit the room, his sons had already made it to the front yard. Who could it be at that time of the evening? The KhAD secret police raided houses mostly during the dark hours. After a forced entry, they conducted a search and took the men of the household away for interrogation, many of whom never returned.

"God have mercy," Sekandar said again as he stepped out of the hallway. Maybe the government was at his doorstep to arrest his sons.

"Who is it?" Jawad called out while walking toward the gate.

"It's me. Hazrat," a high-pitched voice answered from the other side.

"Hazrat, who are you?" Aziz asked.

"I'm from Deh Bala. Commander Daoud has sent me."

The brothers looked at each other. They remembered Daoud, the boy who had fought Sarwar over irrigation water years ago. When that fight happened, nobody was around to break it up. It must have lasted a long time, until Sarwar had drawn his dagger and thrusted it into Daoud's gut. And when he had turned around, leaving him to bleed to death, Daoud had gathered every ounce of whatever energy he had left, and surprised him with a shovel blow on the back of his head. Both boys had laid there for God knows how long before a passerby had noticed them. People said Sarwar was crazy to begin with, but that strike of the shovel had rendered his condition irreversible.

***

Aziz opened the gate, "Salam, Hazrat. Is everything okay?"

A birdcage dangled from the left hand of the small-framed man dressed in black. Although Jawad had met Hazrat before, it has been so long that he could hardly recognize him.

The flickering lantern light exaggerated the depth with which the wrinkles had formed across Hazrat's dust-stricken face. Two ghostly men stood across the street by the river, waiting for him to return. They had concealed their weapons and wrapped their faces with their *pattu*, shawls. The brothers could not identify them, but it was obvious that they were there to protect Hazrat in case trouble arose. Those days, with machineguns slung on so many shoulders, one could never be too careful.

"Salam, Aziz. Commander Daoud sends his respect. He ordered me to return these pigeons to you. He held the cage up. The *Siyah Patains* that have been lost for the past two months quietly sat inside.

"How does he know they are ours?"

"I don't know. I think he heard a rumor from the boys in the village that you are looking for them."

Aziz glanced at his brother. Jawad remained silent letting his Lala, big brother decide.

"Thank you Hazrat. You must have walked a long distance. Come inside. Get some rest, have some tea."

"You are kind. It is getting dark. We have to head back soon," he said, still holding his hand up toward Aziz.

"Give *Qomandan Sayb*, Sir Commander my best and thank him on my behalf. But I can't accept his generosity."

"Why not?"

"You see, once a dove abandons our flock, once it's gone, it's gone forever. We don't take it back. These are nice doves, but they are disloyal. Obviously, they don't want to be in our flock, and I don't want to force them to stay."

84

They are birds, for God's sake. What do they know about loyalty? Hazrat said to himself. He didn't really understand Aziz's way of thinking. But it didn't matter. As far as Hazrat was concerned, he had completed the first part of his mission. So, without further ado, he reached for his vest's side pocket and took out a neatly folded paper, "No problem, I'll take them back. *Qomandan Sayb,* Sir Commander also instructed me to give you this letter."

This time Aziz accepted the offer.

Before Hazrat turned around to join his friends, Jawad called, "Give'm my best."

"*Ba chashm,* definitely."

***

Once inside, Jawad pulled the lantern closer, so he could read the letter aloud.

"*De . . . dear, dear Bro . . . brother.* Bad handwriting. He must have written this with his foot. I am actually surprised Daoud wrote this. He couldn't write his name back then," frustrated, he shot a glance at his audience—Aziz, Sori and Baba.

***

Jawad and Daoud were classmates until fifth grade. Although they hadn't kept in touch for years, together as kids they had climbed on mulberry trees, swum in the river, and shot sparrows with a slingshot. Once, Daoud had even invited him to his compound for lunch. One of the very few times that Jawad had stopped eating because he was full, and not because there was not more to eat. He could never forget that pleasant experience. Food was abundant in Daoud's house, as it was at Sarwar's. After all, their fathers were both *Khans,* chiefs of their respective villages, owning countless acres of land and large herds of cattle.

***

When Baba injured his back on the job, and became hospitalized, Jawad had to drop out of fifth grade to help Aziz with work on the farm. He had promised Sori to accompany her back to school after Baba's recovery, but he never fulfilled that promise. Jawad had realized how hard it was for Baba to work on the land, and he was not going to let his aging father injure himself again. Since then, he had never touched a book or a pencil again.

"Sis, I am too slow. Maybe you could read it," Jawad said, handing the paper to Sori.

Sori hesitantly leaned over and took the letter with a trembling hand. She was going to read aloud a letter written by a man who has been asking for her hand for the past two years. Could there be a mention of her name in it? She felt a flash of heat brushing over her cheeks.

***

Before Sarwar torched the school, many afternoons, during dismissal, Daoud would pretend to be passing by on the other side of the river. After school, Sori would keep her chin up, and maintain a serious expression while walking home. She resented being followed by a creep like Daoud. His behavior could have started rumors about her, shaming her family in the entire village. Most likely, people would have blamed *her* for seducing him. Why would the son of a *Khan,* a powerful landlord chase the daughter of a poor, landless peasant? She didn't know how to get rid of him. If she told her brothers, a feud would break out, and somebody might seriously get hurt or even killed.

Daoud would continue to make it known that he was interested in Sori. Within a year, his mother had made four visits to Sekandar's house, asking for Sori's hand. In response, Sekandar had presented various versions of the same excuse, "My daughter is too young, and she hasn't even finished school yet."

***

The harder Sori clenched the paper, the faster her hands trembled. Trying to convince herself that no one noticed, she kept it about five inches away from her face and began reading with a voice not much louder than a whisper:

"Dear . . . Dear brothers Jawad and Aziz, please accept my Salam and sincere respects—

"Can't you read a little louder? You know my ears are heavy."

"Yes Baba," she said, burying her face deeper into the paper.

"A few weeks ago, your doves got mixed up with my flock. That must have happened for a reason. Maybe this was God's way of bringing us together, because I think of you as my own brothers, and I have great respect for my uncle

Sekandar. Everybody knows that no man is as honorable as you and your father in Deh Darya.

Dear brothers, it has been a year since I have begun my jihad against the communists. The mujahedin of my group are brave men. But I need courageous men like you. Unlike some other people who plunder, burn, and harass civilians, we serve our God and our village, and we actually fight against the Soviets.

Still, what we do is not enough at all. I have some plans to, God willing, defeat the Soviets, and even launch attacks on Kabul. But first, we need to bring this region under a unified command. And for that reason, I need your help. Some people don't, but I do understand the value of brave men like you. I welcome you warmly to join me in my jihad against the infidels. Please take your time and think about my proposal. Our mujahedin are always at your service. 'Wa mennallah-e ttawfiq,' And victory is from God.

Your brother,
Daoud"

Jawad said, "The Soviets have camped out on the mountain slopes. You can see them from the hills. Before reaching Kabul, he has to go through them first."

Aziz reached for the letter, "I think Daoud has other plans. He wants to add territory; he wants to bring everybody under his command. Nobody should know about this. If Sarwar finds out about Daoud's recruiting campaign, there is going to be war," he crumpled and stuffed the paper into his side pocket.

Sori let out a sigh of relief, thinking, *thank God, there was nothing in it about me.* Maybe it was an attempt by Daoud to get close to her by recruiting her brothers to his group first. But, that will never happen. Baba's loyalty lies with Qayoum Khan. He will never let any of his sons join a rival group.

When Sori was reading Daoud's letter, Jawad thought about revealing a decision that he had made two weeks ago.

***

As usual, the men slept in *Bala Khana*, the upper room. Sori could never be able to sleep to the howling of wolves, the wind lashing through the tree branches, and the call of the owls. She preferred to sleep downstairs alone with the door and windows shut throughout the night.

"To tell the truth, I think Daoud has a point," Jawad said, tucking himself under a thin bed sheet.

"What kind of a point?" about to fall asleep, Aziz opened his eyes.

"A point about Sarwar," Jawad pushed his blanket away and sat upright. He had much on his mind and a lot more to say, "Sarwar is not a good *mujahed*, you know. Daoud is right. He *does* harass people."

"Like how?" Baba, too, sat up.

"Like sometimes, he blocks the road and stops cars, beats up some of the passengers, and empties their pockets. He thinks anyone who lives in Kabul, works for the government. Every time this happens, a couple of other guys and I try to stop him, calm him down."

Baba couldn't believe his ears, "This is horrible."

Jawad shook his head, "Sure, Sarwar doesn't think so. In fact, he believes looting these people is a kind of a *jihad*. Because in his eyes they are infidels, they deserve to be looted."

"What does he do with the money?"

"Keeps some, gives the rest to the boys. I made it clear he shouldn't offer that *haram*, prohibited money to me. When he started laughing at me calling the money *haram*, I almost punched him."

For a few seconds, silence loomed with only crickets chirping in the background.

I am going to talk to Qayoum Khan about this," Baba said.

"Qayoum Khan? Just the other day, a whole bunch of RPGs and Kalashnikovs were delivered to Sarwar from Pakistan. Baba, you have to understand. He is not Qayoum Khan's son any more. He is *Commander* Sarwar. He can do whatever he wants."

"No, I must talk to his father. Somebody has to show this boy the right path."

"He'll never change, Baba. If you say something to Khan, Sarwar will blame me for it. He'll hold it against me, and he doesn't like me already."

"What do you mean? Did anything happen between you two?"

"No, nothing."

Aziz jumped in, "You know I haven't crushed you in a long time. Tell the truth."

"Actually we got into a fight," following a pause, Jawad said.

"What? Why didn't you tell me?" Baba roared.

"Well, three days ago I stopped him from beating up a Kabuli school boy. He was about Masih's age. Sarwar started kicking and slapping him because he was carrying a book with a red cover. I didn't know what kind of a book it was. But Sarwar said it was Lenin's book that taught infidelity."

"But he is illiterate. How did he know it was Lenin's book?" Aziz asked.

"Exactly, that's what I was saying. What if the Holy Quran's verses were written in it? Anyway, when I saw blood gushing from that poor lad's nostrils, I jumped in. I told Sarwar *bas,* enough. He was furious. But he knew I would fight him right there and then. So, he stopped."

Angry and astonished, Baba's eyes glowed in the dark, "I must talk to his father."

"No Baba. Please don't do that. If that boy ever disrespects you, I'll kill him."

"Jawad is right. We have to keep our distance from them until things cool down," Aziz said.

"I don't know about you, brother, but I don't think my situation will ever improve with that loser. I just can't stand him anymore."

"What do you mean, Jawad?"

"I want to get out of his team."

"What are you going to do? Join Daoud's group?"

"No. If I do that, Sarwar would harass you all the time. I just don't want any trouble with him anymore. Qayoum Khan has done so much for us, makes it hard to beat up his son."

"You have to stay with him. You don't have a choice," Baba said.

Jawad looked up, fixing his gaze at the ceiling in the utter darkness, "I have thought about this a lot. Maybe it is better—"

"Better to do what?" Aziz asked, "hide in the well when he comes knocking? You know he will. He wants one of us around."

"No, maybe it is better if I leave the village, go to Pakistan," Jawad muttered.

Baba Sekandar pulled a matchbox from under his mattress and lit the lantern sitting by the window. Under the pale glow of the flame, he could see the grief in his son's eyes, "What are you going to do in Pakistan, son? Millions of people are rotting in refugee camps over there. Don't you hear it in the news?"

Every night, Baba and his sons listened to BBC or Voice of America on their battery run, transistor radio to track *mujahedin's* progress on various fronts around the country.

"I know Baba. Life is not easy in Pakistan. But what can I do? If I go to Kabul, I will either end up with the army or in Pul-e Charkhi," the infamous jailhouse from which thousands of political prisoners never came out alive. Jawad sighed after saying what he had been planning to say for the past two weeks.

Dumbfounded, Aziz stared at his brother's saddened young face. What would happen to him in that strange land? Would he ever see him again? He understood Jawad's anxiety. Based on what he had heard, he too no longer wanted to cooperate with Sarwar. He would definitely stay away from him and his so-called *jihad*. But, if Sarwar ever came knocking, Aziz would have to follow his lead.

"Go son. May God keep you safe and healthy wherever you may be," Reluctantly, Sekandar gave him his blessing.

***

A week later, on a cold spring evening, Jawad said goodbye to his family. To affirm his respect for the man he loved and admired throughout his life, he kissed his father's hands for the last time.

Sori pressed her forehead against her brother's chest, "God is kind. One day, there will be peace in Afghanistan, and you will come back."

"*Bad az har tariki roshanist,* there is light after every darkness," Jawad planted a kiss on her face. Then, he hugged his brother and began to walk toward Deh Bala, where Commander Daoud and his men awaited his arrival. Daoud would personally accompany and guide him all the way to Pakistan as he had promised.

As Baba, Sori, and Aziz looked on, gradually Jawad' silhouette disappeared like a shadow among all other shadows in the dark.

THIRTEEN

"**M**ay I come in? Masih knocked three times on the Student Services Department door and waited for a response from the stocky, mustached man, sitting behind a metal desk on the far end of the office. He was the man who had muddled Masih's name on his student identification card.

"Come in *rafiq*, comrade," he said, glancing up for a split second. He seemed busy writing on one of the papers piled on his desk. His thick mustache, solid black eyebrows, and dark brown eyes, combined with a serious tone of voice helped him project a solemn presence.

Masih eased into the office and gently placed his application on the man's desk, as if it was a sheet of glass. The man looked up again and said, "One minute." Then he delved right back into whatever he was writing.

The sun beamed in through a wide window behind him, warming up the small office more than necessary. Similar windows surrounded Habibia high school's four-story building with nicely tiled floors and high ceilings.

Masih stepped back and waited. He cautiously looked around. To his left, a portrait of President Babrak Karmal hung on the wall. He was the new Shah Shuja of modern Afghanistan. According to Father, the British colonialists had installed their puppet, King Shuja a few decades ago to rule on their behalf. Now the Soviets have chosen Karmal as their dummy. A large rectangular red cloth dangled from the opposite wall. On it, a skillful calligrapher had inscribed three powerful words, stretching from one end to the other, '*Nan, Lebas, Khana*, Food, Clothing, Shelter. That was the regime's mantra, a simple slogan consisting of the most basic human needs, of which many Afghans were deprived, and on which the Marxists hoped to capitalize.

About five long minutes later, the man put down his pen and picked up Masih's application. He stared at it for a few seconds. It was written in two short paragraphs. Masih had explained that a *talashi*, officer had ripped his I.D. and therefore he was in immediate need of another.

The man scanned the application and looked up, "You've written it yourself?"

"Yes sir," Masih said politely and hoped that he would not point out any spelling or grammatical errors, making him rewrite the whole thing. *Maybe I should have let Mother write it.*

"What grade?"

"Tenth, sir."

"Huh, tenth grade? You have done a good job. Your writing is better than many twelve graders," he looked at the application again, and then shifted his gaze to Masih's nervous face. "What did you do wrong comrade? Why did they rip your I.D.?"

"Nothing sir, I did nothing wrong." If anybody, it was the comrade himself who had done something wrong, jumbling up his first and last name. Now, however, was not the time to argue over who was at fault for Masih's situation. His only goal was to walk away with a new I.D. in his pocket. If he had to, he would even promise never to bother the comrade again. This time, however, he better write Masih's name and his father's name correctly.

"You haven't lost it, have you?" he gave Masih a suspicious look.

Why was he asking that question? Was he looking for an excuse not to issue the document? What difference did it make, if it was stolen or eaten by a dog? Masih needed an I.D. and it was this man's responsibility to issue him one.

"No sir," he produced the pieces that he had glued together from the back pocket of his discolored jeans, and leaned forward, holding it up so the man could see it.

"If they catch you with this artistic piece, they'll automatically send you to a warfront in Khost province," he finished his sentence erupting into a full belly laughter.

Unable to understand the humor in his statement, Masih waited for him to finish, "That's why I'm applying for a—"

"I know, I know," the man jumped in, holding the palm of his hand up, "I know why you are here. What I don't know is whether you are a member?"

A member? "A member of what?"

With elbows pinned on the desk, he crossed his fingers under his chin, "A member of the People Democratic Party's Youth Organization." By now, he had stopped laughing.

The comrade was talking about the organization that prepared the youth to become the Marxists of the future.

"No, I'm not," he answered.

"Why not?"

"I don't have time to attend their meetings," sheepishly, Masih placed the tattered I.D. back in his pocket. True, he may not have done a good job in making him believe in the veracity of the excuse that he had just blurted out. Yet, compared to what he actually wanted to say, *I am not a traitor like you, and I hate your organization,* his answer didn't sound too bad.

"You should make time. The revolution needs capable youths like you," said the comrade, scribbling a couple of lines on the bottom of the application, and returning the paper to Masih. "Go upstairs to the Organization's office. Get the secretary's signature. Then, bring it back to me, and I'll issue you a new I.D."

A simple question kept spinning in Masih's mind. *Why would the mustached comrade need the secretary's signature in order to issue me a simple student I.D.?* But he didn't take the risk to ask. The man didn't seem to be having a pleasant day to begin with. Better not to say anything that might put him on the defensive. The document was literally Masih's license to live. If it required an extra signature, so be it.

All he had to do was to follow the comrade's order—go upstairs and get a signature, no problem. He thanked him and hurried out.

Leaping toward the marble-tiled staircases, he glanced at the bottom of his application and stopped. The man's handwriting was neat and artistic—the *nastaliq* style:

Comrade Secretary, I am referring comrade Masih Sharif to you. Please take the necessary steps to ensure his participation and notify our office so we can renew his I.D.

He had signed his name as Tofan, meaning storm. *The necessary steps?* What was that supposed to mean? Definitely not a good thing, and most likely, a glitch in the process. Well, he would just have to go to the organization's directorate and find out.

***

The office was a rectangular-shaped room with no windows, gloomy and smaller than Tofan's space. A dark oak desk, almost as wide as the room itself, occupied the far end of it. Behind it, there sat a muscular man, who seem to be in his mid-twenties. His carefully shaved head caught Masih's attention. Mostly, those drafted into the army shaved their heads like that. Why would any young man in his right mind want to be bald? But then again, anything was possible and expected from a communist. If he was crazy enough to sell his country to the Soviets, he could do many other things that would not make sense. As Masih stepped forward, he realized that the man's face seemed familiar. For sure, he had seen him somewhere, maybe around the school or elsewhere. He just couldn't remember where he had met him before.

On the left side of the office, there sat three boys on chairs arranged in a row against the wall. As he moved forward to approach the secretary's desk, the boys stopped their group conversation and stared at Masih.

"Mr. Tofan asked me to get your signature on this. *Talashi* ripped my I.D. I need to get another one," he said, slowly placing the application along with the battered I.D. on his desk.

The secretary picked up the paper, skimmed through it, and asked, "What did comrade Tofan say to you?" He let go of the paper. It landed on the desk.

"He said I need your signature, so he could issue me a new I.D."

"I will sign your application, but you have to follow the procedure, meet the condition, you know."

"Mr. Tofan didn't say anything about a condition."

"Well, I'm telling you," he said, pointing his thumb toward his own chest, "I can't sign this unless you become a member."

"Member? Member of what?" he asked, hearing a chuckle from one of the boys. The secretary was referring to the membership of no other organization, but the one Masih had just stepped into.

He answered with a smirk on his face, "Come on Masih. You know what I'm talking about, the Democratic Youth Organization of Afghanistan."

Masih realized why he had asked that useless question—to buy time while searching for an excuse to reject his invitation. It would have to be believable as well as acceptable. It must show that it was impossible for him to take on this new responsibility. Of course, the real excuse was that he didn't want to be part of an organization related to those responsible for the arrest of his father. In fact, he would rather take up arms against those cowards who sold their *namoos,* honor to the Soviets; he would rather join Jawad and Aziz on the mountains to help free his father from captivity and his country from occupation.

But he couldn't say anything along those lines. The slightest complaint or hint of displeasure would get him expelled from school, and even land him in prison.

Then how could he offer a satisfactory answer to this miserable bald man? He couldn't just say, *no thank you, I am not interested.* This man was going to demand a reasonable explanation as to why Masih was not joining this 'great' institution. And if he could come up with a convincing answer, he had to state it without revealing his feelings of disgust about the organization and the ideology it promoted.

The words of Mulla Salim echoed in his mind. *O, people! Beware! Whoever cooperates with this government is a Kafer,* infidel. By becoming a member, Masih would not only have to live with that disgrace throughout his life, but he will also burn in hell in the afterlife.

He tried, but couldn't swallow his saliva. In fact, there was no saliva to swallow. His pounding heart had found a fist of its own. He remembered feeling the same way when the soldier had ordered him to climb into the truck. But yesterday, as he had learned from

Mother, Khalifa Zaman was there to save him. Who was going to come to his rescue today?

"I am not ready now. Can I join some other time?"

"No. You have to join now. This is not a soccer team. This is the *Youth Organization*. If you sign up now, you'll get your I.D. issued in about ten minutes. What do you say, huh?"

Masih wished he could wipe the sweat off the back of his neck and forehead. Meanwhile, what the man said struck him with a realization. He had watched him many times defending the Afghan national soccer team's goal post. Masih had heard from his classmates that they had seen Bital around the campus, and that he was some sort of a representative from Kabul University. Apparently, he was a lot more than that. Bital was the head of the Democratic Youth Organization of Afghanistan in Habibia high school in addition to being one of the best goalkeepers of the country's national soccer team.

Now Masih remembered the brave defender tumbling under the galloping feet of Russian, Uzbek, and Mongolian opponents in Ghazi National Stadium. During most of those matches, the offense of the other team would gang up on him, taking shots at his goal post from all sorts of angles. But Bital would stand strong and deflect more than ninety percent of the strikes. Every time he dove in to snatch the ball in mid-air, the crowd in the packed stadium rose to their feet, clapped, and whistled in a deafening frenzy as if their team had already won. Among them, Masih and Father too would proudly applaud, jump to their feet, and cheer. Excited and ecstatic, they had witnessed Bital deny victory to the foreigners time after time.

Yet sometimes, even deflecting ninety-nine percent of the strikes did not guarantee a victory for Afghanistan. Once in a while, the strikes that did make it through produce more goals than the Afghans could score. Because of this, on the way home from the stadium, Masih and Father would not talk to each other or laugh as much as they did when they left the house. But they would never lose hope. Next time, their team would perform better. This optimism drove them back to the stadium again and again.

"Even if our team loses a thousand times, we should support them. They are capable of winning," Dr. Sharif would say to his son. He was sure that if the Afghans discovered a few more players like Homayoun-e *Raaket,* The Rocket, Rajab Ali *Dewana,* the Crazy, and

Samad-e *Bital*, the Beatle, Afghanistan would be able to shine on the international stage.

Occasionally, when they did win, fans would jump on their feet, screaming, and exchanging hugs and kisses. Sometimes, the ecstatic crowd would rush into the field and carry a superstar like Bital on their shoulders for a victory lap.

Masih could not believe his eyes, realizing that he was not only standing in the presence of one of the best soccer players in the country, but also conversing with him.

He loved the game, but was terrible at playing it. He had tried a few times, but on every occasion when the ball had touched his foot, in a daze of confusion he had lost the ability to distinguish left from right. He had no idea to whom to pass the ball. And when he did manage to kick it, the pass would almost never make it to another teammate. A boy like Masih could only dream of speaking to a man like Bital.

***

Sitting behind the desk, Bital seemed a lot calmer than the way he acted when he stood on guard in front of the country's goal post. On the field, as the captain of his team, he would yell and make frantic hand gestures, expressing his anger and frustration at his teammates. Here though, he sat behind the desk in total control, his lips slightly curved into a faint smile while he studied the skinny boy standing in front of him.

"Comrade Masih, answer my question. I don't have a lot of time."

"Well," Masih said, sounding unsure of what he was about to say, "the problem is, my mother is ill, my father has been missing, and this year I have to start studying for the university entrance exam."

"Joining us doesn't take that much time. All you have to do is attend a meeting once in a while."

Masih thought hard, but did not have enough time to come up with another excuse. Besides, he had already used the best excuses he could think of all at once.

"If you could please sign my application, I will be grateful to you. Please give me a day to think about your offer and ask my mother for permission," he said, wishing he could candidly tell what he really thought about him and his shameful organization.

Despite being a national hero, Bital was nothing but a traitor. And what mattered the most was who he was, not what his athletic feats were. He was a man who had betrayed his country, and even though Masih was bad at soccer, thank God, he was not a coward and an infidel like him. Thank God, unlike Bital, he did have a conscience.

Bital refused to be convinced. This boy was not presenting a genuine explanation for his delay in taking advantage of such a great opportunity. But the goalie had secured him in his grip and was not going to let go.

"What if your mother didn't let you join us?"

All swinging eyes, shifting back and forth between the two, turned to Masih. The tight windowless room began to seem even smaller and hotter than it felt when Masih had initially entered. The best answer he could think of was "I don't know."

"What is your rank in the class?"

"I ranked third last year," he said. Thank God, Bital had changed the subject. He had ranked first and second every year except for ninth grade. Since his father's detention, Masih's standing had dropped to third. But, what his academic performance had to do with him being issued a simple document?

"Look Masih, you seem to be a smart boy," Bital said with a soft tone, leaning forward, "we have a need to recruit bright-minded young men like yourself. You know, boys like you could one day become great leaders."

"It is very kind of you, but no sir, I'm not as smart as you say."

"Now are you being humble, or just making excuses?"

Masih knew that he was a bad liar, but he continued to insist, "I am not making any excuses."

"I think you are. I just hope that it is not because you are under the influence of the enemy's propaganda. Do you know what will happen to this country, to this party if young men like you didn't act right now?" The enemy injects all kinds of garbage into the brains of our youth, so they too become the servants of the Pakistanis, Arabs, and the Americans. Today, if the great Soviet Army didn't help us, the imperialists would have already destroyed our country. How long are we going to look at our Soviet comrades to defend *our* country? This is a big *nang,* disgrace. Let's stand against the imperialists. Let's defend our *namoos*, honor. The same way our fathers defeated the British, we too should teach the Americans a lesson.

Bital finished his last sentence with the thumping sound of a pounding fist on the desk. Masih didn't know how to respond to that heap of emotional arguments that Bital had poured on him at once. He hoped that the boys sitting on his left didn't hear the loud beating of his racing heart.

Bital looked up at a framed portrait of President Babrak Karmal on the right hand wall, and read a quote by him, inscribed bellow his photo, "Youth are the Architects of Afghanistan's Future." He remained silent for a few seconds to give the boys time to ponder the depth of the statement. Then he said, "If the young generation refuses to play an active role in politics, how are we going to shape the future of this country?"

He was right. The youth should play an active role in politics, but not on his side of the fence. His mini-speech raised a few questions in Masih's mind. How could he claim that the Americans were attacking Afghanistan, while the soldiers roaming around the streets were Soviets? And why would these invaders, who didn't believe in God, want to help the Afghans who were Muslims? They must have had a hidden agenda. According to Father, their goal was to enslave the Afghans and expand their territory all the way to the shores of the Indian Ocean. Finally, what did the issuance of a simple I.D. have to do with joining the organization, American imperialism, and the Soviet benevolence anyway? *Why can't he simply sign the damn paper and send me on my way?*

However, he decided not to add to Bital's anger with any of the questions spinning in his head. Instead, he offered a hopeful idea, "I want to serve my country in the future." Giving him this assurance could calm him down. Then Masih wouldn't have to tolerate listening to the rest of his speech.

"How are you going to do that? You need the courage to start somewhere, and joining the organization would definitely be a good first step."

"I *do* have the courage," the slight vibration in Masih's voice, combined with the austerity in which he responded indicated that he did not like the offensive implication. Masih was not frightened; he was disgusted with all the lies upon which the organization was founded. "I actually want to become an architect so I can help build Afghanistan in the future."

"Well, that's nice. With all the destruction around us, this country needs great builders. But at the same time, you can be a member of the party, building the political future of Afghanistan. Look at me. I work here *and* am studying to be a lawyer. And still, I end up with spare time to play soccer once in a while," he said, flashing a smile that revealed his perfectly arranged sparkling teeth.

Masih had no ammunition left in his arsenal of excuses except to say, "Can I think about it?"

After a glance at his watch, Bital produced a blank paper from his desk drawer and began scribbling on it with a shiny fountain pen. Then he signed at the bottom of the sheet, and pounded the organization's official stamp next to it.

"Here, show this to any search officer. Tell them Bital signed it. They'll let you go. I will give you a day to make your decision. I hope it's going to be a wise one."

Desperately wanting to get out of that suffocating chamber, he whispered, "Thank you."

***

Despite the fact that Masih had already stepped out of the office, he didn't feel liberated at all. He just realized that Tofan had kicked him like a soccer ball to his goalkeeper comrade upstairs. Bital had clawed his fingers around his neck, and Masih knew that freeing himself was not going to be easy. But the thought that angered him the most was that Bital had vehemently argued in favor of the invaders, *and* he had expected Masih to believe in his nonsense. In effect, he was asking Masih to forget about his conscience, religion, and the fact that the regime had kidnapped and jailed his father.

As he passed through the vacant hallway and stepped down the staircase, through one of the wide windows, he saw a large flock of birds flying toward the Sher Darwaza Mountain. He stopped and smiled. Then, remembering his pigeons, he rushed down the steps. As he exited the building, his fast-paced walk transformed into a slow jog, and then a sprint. He had to hurry. Mother must have been worried, and the birds starving.

FOURTEEN

"**D**on't worry, I already took care of them," said Mother, watching Masih run toward the cage in the hallway.

He stopped, "Thanks, I was worried about them."

Nadia could tell he was embarrassed, "And I was worried about *you*. Where were you? You know, you should have left them with a lot more food and water."

"I am sorry."

"Don't apologize to me. Ask them for forgiveness. I hope this doesn't happen again. You know it's wrong," she headed for the kitchen, "come on, dinner is ready."

The events of the day had made him lose his appetite. But once he entered the kitchen, the steam rising from *shorba*, the beef stew made him realize he was actually starving. He sat on the seat that Father used to occupy, one of the four metal chairs around the square-shaped table.

Placing a bowl in front of him, Nadia said, "Careful, hot," followed by, "did you renew your I.D.?"

On the way home, he had thought about conjuring up an answer to the inevitable question, but he had not been able to formulate one.

"Not yet," Masih said, staring at the aromatic steam that lifted from the bowl. Then, he picked up a slice of bread and began to shred it into the broth.

"Not yet? What do you mean not yet?"

"The secretary of the Youth Organization has to sign the application. Then they'll issue it."

"So? Have him sign it," she said, setting another bowl on her side of the table.

"I will. I just have to give him an appeal that explains how I lost my I.D.," he shamelessly lied.

"I will help you write one."

"Thanks Mother, I don't need your help. I already wrote one."

"Then why hasn't he signed it? Is there anything wrong with it?"

"Of course not. There is nothing wrong with my application," he said, sounding frustrated.

A few times in the past, Nadia had caught her son in similar situations, where he had not been able to substitute the truth with a believable lie. This time, however, he was speaking with much more confidence. The hesitation apparent in his voice six months ago seemed undetectable today.

"You should have gotten that signature," Nadia said.

"I tried, but the guy wasn't there. He wasn't in his office," shamelessly, he lied again. But what could he have done? Tell her that he was about to join the Marxist Youth Organization? Isn't it a part of the same government that raided their house and arrested his father? If Masih joined the Youth Organization, neither himself, nor Mother could do anything about it—another valid reason for not telling her the truth. Perhaps he could break the news after Father's release from the prison.

"When is this man coming to the office, did you ask?"

"I don't know, maybe tomorrow."

"So what's going to happen? If tomorrow on your way to school, the search forces catch you again with those torn pieces of paper, they will take you away. This time, Khalifa Zaman is not going to be there to save your life."

"I know," he had to prevent himself from telling her about Bital's proposition, "Mother, don't worry, I will get the signature tomorrow, okay. It's not a big deal." His beef stew had disappeared under the shredded bread pile.

Nadia stepped toward the pressure cooker that sat on a kerosene stove in the corner. With her back toward him, she pleaded to God to hail His wrath upon the communists. She mumbled a few more expletives, and Masih heard every one of them.

"Mother, don't stress. Everything is going to be alright."

"How can I not? Tomorrow I am going with you to school. I want to make sure that this man signs your application."

Mother had no idea that Masih did not have an application, nor did he have a student I.D. Bital had confiscated both and slipped them into his desk drawer.

"You could do nothing, and if you come to school, everyone will make fun of me. You are going to embarrass me, Mother."

"You must get that I.D. issued tomorrow. Do you understand?"

"Mother, I *will*," Masih paused, and stared at the untouched meal. "If not, then maybe we could move to Deh Darya."

While taking her first bite, Nadia's hand froze before reaching her mouth. "What? Have you lost your mind? What about your school?"

"I will go to school later, but now I want to be a *mujahed*, fighter."

For a couple of seconds, Nadia's mouth remained open, no longer waiting for the bite.

"*Bachem*, my son," she always said *bachem* prior to a lecture. You have plenty of time to become one. Right now, your *jihad* is to study so one day, just like your father, you can serve your country."

"Mother, first of all, I am not a child. I am *fifteen* now. Secondly, going to school is not going to free this country. It is not a *jihad*. If it were, Mulla Salim wouldn't have asked people not to go to school anymore. He said so. I heard him with my own ears. He is a Mulla, and obviously he knows more than you do."

"Thousands of boys are dying in this war, and I don't want you to be one of them. There are other ways for you to serve your country."

"Come on Mother, let's not kid ourselves. *Jihad* is to fight against the Soviets, not to ignore everything, go to school, and get brainwashed by the communists."

Nadia clinched her teeth, "No, going to school *is* jihad, and you made a promise to your father to take care of me and finish your education. How can you do those things if you waste your precious youth   wandering   around   the   mountains?"

"Of course, I will take care of you. I will take care of you even if I didn't make a promise to Father. But Mother, how *can* I go to school knowing that the Soviets have invaded our country, that the government has jailed my father? Do you want me to accept this kind of *be-ghairati*, disgrace?"

What a stubborn boy, just like his father. She raised her hands as if she was addressing God. "It's simple! You go to school, you study hard, and you graduate. That's how. You graduate first. After that, you will be responsible for your own decisions."

"If all guys go to university like me, and forget that they have been enslaved by the Soviets, then who is going to defend this country? Who is going to kick the Soviets out?"

"If every schoolboy becomes a *mujahed*, and every educated man like your father disappears, what's going to happen to the future of this country? Afghanistan doesn't need only warriors. We have more than enough of them. We also need doctors, teachers, and engineers. Remember, in this country not just any kid gets the opportunity to become one."

"For as long as we are invaded, nobody has a future in Afghanistan. After college, my faith and my future would be just like Father."

"I am *not*," Nadia shouted, slapping both hands on the table, "going to let *anybody* steal you from me. Do you understand?" her dark brown eyes widened, beaming with fury as streams of tears rolled down her cheeks. "Don't *ever* say that. You are everything I have," she pushed those words out through her choking throat. Then, she covered her face with her hands.

Masih couldn't think of anything to say. There were no words to alleviate Mother's pain. Sorrow and guilt of making her cry lay heavy on his heart. He had no choice but to obtain that I.D., even if it meant to give up his dream of becoming a warrior; or worse, to join the enemy. He made a promise to himself. *I'll never let her suffer again.*

FIFTEEN

As the sun began to disappear behind the mountains surrounding Kabul, someone rang the doorbell. Nadia opened the gate and saw a man, probably an inch or two shorter than Dr. Sharif, standing on the sidewalk. He was nervously looking over his shoulders to the left and right. As he stepped forward to greet Nadia, she realized that he looked familiar.

"*Salam,* Hello," he said, removing his sunglasses to reveal his tired eyes, "sister, I am Dr. Yawar. I don't know if you remember me. But I was a classmate of Dr. Sharif. It was a while ago. Back then, you were studying in the School of Literature."

"Yes, you look very familiar. Sorry, my son is not home, but he will be here soon," Nadia tacitly explained why she could not invite him inside for a cup of tea.

"No problem sister. I understand. I just need to talk to you about Sharif in private," he flung a quick glance over his shoulder before stepping in. She shut the door behind him.

"Do you have any news from Sharif?" Nadia could no longer wait.

"Sister, Dr. Sharif was one of my good friends throughout my years at Kabul University. For a few months, we even shared a room in the hostel. I knew him well enough to say that he was an honorable man."

"Have you heard anything about him?" Nadia began to weep as if she already knew what Dr. Yawar was about to say.

"I am really sorry. I am afraid I don't have good news."

"What kind of news?" the thought of the response she was going to receive drew every drop of her blood into her heart. She placed her right hand over it as if to prevent it from leaping out of her chest. And to maintain her balance on her trembling legs, she reached for the doorknob.

"Sister, your husband has attained the highest of all ranks, martyrdom. I am sorry. I couldn't save him. May his soul rest in peace."

For the past forty-eight hours, Dr. Yawar has been thinking about the least painful way to deliver the heart-wrenching news to Sharif's wife. He had not been able to find one.

Nadia's hand slipped off the doorknob as her body slammed onto the concrete pathway. She tried, but couldn't scream, couldn't make a sound. Since the night of her husband's arrest, she had had many nightmares. Now, all of them were coming true.

"No, no, why?" that was all she could muster to push through her choked throat.

As she sobbed, Dr. Yawar sat next to her, reached into the inside pocket of his jacket and produced a small item wrapped in a white fabric. Holding it in his palm, he unfolded the cloth with the other trembling hand to disclose a pair of reading glasses, one lens missing and the other shattered.

Through a blurred vision, Nadia recognized the spectacles. She kissed, smelled, and rubbed the broken pieces against her eyes.

He said, "May God grant you patience. There is nothing I could say to ease your pain."

Dr. Yawar had fulfilled his moral responsibility. Sharif's wife had the right to know, and as a doctor and a friend it was his duty to tell her the truth.

The secret service, KhAD had realized that Dr. Sharif was serving as a propaganda machine for the *mujahedin*. Somehow, they had to shut him up. Yet, they didn't want to kill him. That would have been too risky, bad publicity for the government. Instead, they decided to give him a *gosh-mali*, an ear rubbing. Unfortunately, during the 'interrogation,' an inexperienced agent had tried too hard to make him talk and to impress his boss. He had employed too much brutal force on the detainee, weighing only 145 pounds. This occurred after Dr. Sharif refused to sign a piece of paper, stating that he regretted every negative comment he had made about the government and that he will never speak ill of the regime again. That was not a promise he could make or keep.

***

"Where, where is his body? For God's sake, where is he?"

"I don't know sister. I swear I don't know. They don't tell me these things. If I ask, they will shoot me. I found his glasses in one of his pockets and saved them, gambling with my life. That was all I could do."

"Where do you work? I will go there and find him myself."

"I work at Charsad-Bestar, the Four-Hundred-Bed hospital. But they did not bring him there. They have their own secret facility. They blindfolded me when they took me there."

***

The night before Dr. Sharif's death, the guards had transferred Dr. Yawar to an undisclosed location to, as they put it, 'attend to the prisoner's medical needs.' He was stunned to find his friend lying unconscious on a cot in an otherwise empty room. He was dying, and Yawar could do nothing to save him. He could probably treat Sharif's fractured right hand and battered legs; he could have stitched the gushing wound above his right eyebrow and beneath his left eye and the splinters on his swollen lips. But what about his internal bleeding? Even if the doctor had the equipment to operate on him, not a trace of strength was left in Sharif's body to pull him through the operation.

***

Nadia asked, "How do I find him?"

"Sister, his body could be anywhere, but his soul is with God, in heaven. Anything you do to find him could jeopardize your own, your son's, and even my life. If the news of his martyrdom spreads, the government will come after me. I am probably the only outsider who knows the truth about him. You don't know these people. I have seen what they are capable of doing to another human being. To them, human life means nothing. If you raise your voice, they will have no mercy on you or on me and my family."

"I am grateful to you, but I wish I could see him just one more time and put his body to rest," Nadia said.

"I understand. But please sister, promise me. Promise that you won't tell anyone about me, or about what you heard from me."

"I promise," Nadia said with tearful eyes.

***

"Mother, are you okay?"

"I am not feeling well," was the only answer she could devise to answer Masih's question.

Nadia sat on her bed and held the broken glasses in her trembling hands. As she sobbed, through glared vision, she noticed a speck wedged between the frame of the left rim and the remaining shred of the glass. She wiped her eyes with the back of her hand and slid across the bed, leaning closer toward the lit candle on the side table. This time, she reexamined it under the light. A blot of ink, maybe? To be sure, she pulled the side table's drawer, and reached for a magnifying glass with which Sharif used to read the fine prints on medication labels.

After about a minute of carefully examining the spot, Nadia was certain of its color—red. It was blood. What else could a red spot, stuck on the broken frame of glasses belonging to a man tortured to death mean? The idea of convincing herself otherwise seemed absurd.

***

Dr. Yawar did not want Sharif's widow to see even a speck of her husband's blood, which would provoke a thousand terrifying thoughts in her mind. With trembling fingers, he had washed and rubbed the bloodstains off the glasses as thorough as he could in one of the abandoned rooms that used to be a lab of some sort. But amidst the anxiety and the dread of possibly being caught, he had missed a tiny spot identifiable with a magnifying glass.

Rumors were widespread about KhAD's brutal methods of interrogation. A political prisoner would be considered lucky to get away with a few sleepless nights, a couple of broken bones, and a few bruises on a disfigured face.

Distressing thoughts and disturbing visions assaulted Nadia's mind throughout the night. She buried her face into the pillow and took a long, deep breath. She could still detect the faint sweet scent of Sharif's cologne.

***

While Nadia was a student at the Literature Faculty of Kabul University, Sharif was working on his medical degree. Shortly after being introduced to her through friends, he succeeded in acquiring a scholarship to study abroad. Prior to his departure, he had obtained a promise from Nadia not to marry any of the other interested boys, and to wait for his return. As a reminder, he had given her a diamond ring, which she had to hide from her family and friends until his return and a formal proposal. The wait lasted four years, but it was well worth it. The day of Sharif's return was one of the happiest days of their life.

In fact, Sharif and Nadia had shared many happy days—the days of watching Indian movies in cinemas around the city, the many Fridays spent picnicking in Paghman's gardens, the day of their formal engagement, their wedding day, and the day Masih was born. For the remainder of the days, they were just happy to be together.

***

She would sob, fall asleep, dream about Sharif, wake up, and repeat the cycle throughout the night.

He comes home from work in a white robe, plants a kiss on her cheek, picks little Masih up and plants another kiss on his chubby cheek—juicy and loud. 'I am beat. Could somebody give me a cup of tea please?' He says with an irresistible pleading tone. Now, he is sitting across the dining table, listening to and smiling at his wife. Finally, he lays on the bed, reading and slowly drifting into sleep—a long peaceful sleep.

Nadia continues to weep silently. Masih must not find out, although one day he will, but now is not the time. If he discovers that the government has killed his father, he will spend the rest of his life seeking revenge. He will not be able to focus on school. He will end up on the mountains of Deh Darya with Jawad and Aziz. Yes, Masih has the right to know. But he also has the right to live, to marry and have children, to have a future.

The communists had deprived Sharif of the right to live. They had stolen Nadia's husband. She will do everything in her power to prevent them from depriving her son of the right to live, from snatching him away too. No. She was not going to let that happen. She must protect him at any cost, even if it means keeping him from learning the truth about his father.

She must hide the broken eyeglasses from Masih. Meanwhile, at sunrise, she would have to seek help from the only person she could trust.

SIXTEEN

Nadia lay awake and watched the clock that sat on her bedside table until it hit 5:00 AM. Then she put on her slippers and light-blue teaching robe, strapping its flimsy belt around her waist. Fearing that Masih might wake up before her return, she tiptoed out of the house and dashed uphill for Khalifa Zaman's house. The morning breeze had died out, and the air felt damp and cold. Men in ragged clothes exited their houses and silently strolled downhill, heading toward the bus stop.

***

"Is everything okay?" confused, Khalifa asked. While he could hardly open his own eyes, the dark circles around Nadia's bloodshot eyes stirred fear in his heart. As far as he could remember, no one had ever shown up at his doorstep at that hour of the day.

Gasping, she forced the words with a scratchy voice, "Help me, Khalifa. They killed my husband."

The news of Dr. Sharif's death shook him and brought tears to his eyes. What he had suspected and feared all along, turned out to be true.

"Your husband is a martyr. He gave his life for this country, for truth. May his soul rest in heaven. Come in sister. Let's pray for him."

Nadia stepped inside, and they raised their hands. Khalifa recited a long verse from the Holy Quran. Nadia listened and cried.

***

Khalifa Zaman knew Sharif ever since his engagement to Nadia. The couple made frequent trips to Deh Darya in his vehicle. After Sharif's return from America, Khalifa sought treatment for his family only from Dr. Sharif. Sometimes, the family would meet him at his office in Kot-e Sangi, a relatively poor neighborhood in the city, while other times they would show up at his house. The men would usually chat over a few cups of green tea. Sharif never feared expressing his political opinions and stood firm for what he believed in. An *eshq*, a passion for truth breathed life into his mind and soul. Had the communists killed that passion within him, the doctor would have already been dead.

The men never failed to argue about politics. Even if both agreed on a point, they would find a way to debate. Often, in the midst of a heated discussion, Khalifa would start coughing heavily, a smoker's cry for help, according to Dr. Sharif.

"How many times have I told you?" he would admonishingly say, "You have to quit. Your lungs are falling apart."

"I am okay. I am just battling a flu," Zaman would answer with a mischievous smile, "and you too Doc, you need to keep some of your opinions to yourself. You know what they say. Walls have mice, and mice have ears. Nobody cares about my opinions, but you are a doctor; people are watching you."

Sharif would smile and recite his favorite verse:

Faash megoyam o azgofta-e khod del shaadam
Barda-e eshqam o az har do jahan azaadam
I tell the truth and am pleased with what I say
I am enslaved to love and free from both worlds

That evening, Khalifa decided to return from work two hours earlier than usual. He swept his vehicle and wiped the seats. Then he sat behind the wheel and drove to Nadia's house.

"Baba is not feeling well. I am delivering some medicine to him. Tomorrow is Friday, so I thought I should stop by and see if you guys want to visit him," Khalifa said when Masih answered the door.

Traveling to the village that late sounded strange. But Masih was always up for a trip to Deh Darya, especially on a bus chartered only for him and his mother.

As the trip began, darkness hovered, leaving Khalifa at the mercy of the vehicle's faint headlights. It inched along, making its way up the graveled road to the village. Nadia sat on the seat behind Khalifa. The shattered reading glasses lay hidden in its case, tucked away in the black leather handbag on her lap. Masih sat next to her, unaware of the real reason behind their travel to Deh Darya. Mother seemed lost in her thoughts as if she had forgotten to breathe, and her forearms tightly circled the black bag. Maybe Baba was battling a serious illness.

The vehicle continued to push forward. Shadows drifted inside the bus while silence loomed outside. Except for a dense ghostlike cloud of dust, floating in front of the headlights, darkness had concealed all shapes and colors, including the daggered peaks of the Hindu Kush and the green valleys on its footsteps.

In honor of Dr. Sharif, Khalifa Zaman tried his best to drive at a steady, graceful pace. He considered it a privilege to be taking him to Deh Darya for the last time and to his final resting place. With eyes fixed on the road, Khalifa reached for a pack of cigarettes, placed a stick between his lips, and flipped the lighter on. This was one of the few times in his life that he had felt such strong urge for a smoke. He stared at the flame and remembered Sharif's argument: *You need to give up this poison. If you stopped smoking today, I guarantee, in six months you will be ten years younger.*

Out of respect, Khalifa always tried not to smoke in front of Dr. Sharif, and especially tonight, it would be impolite to smoke in his presence. He shut the lighter, slipped it back into his pocket, and tossed the cigarette out of the window.

***

Jawad and Aziz had prepared their tools—two shovels and a pickaxe. As soon as the son descended, they began to dig a grave wide, long, and deep enough to fit the actual body of the martyr. That morning, Khalifa had stopped by Baba's house and delivered the news that the government had martyred Dr. Sharif. He had also conveyed Nadia's wish to prepare for a secret funeral for her husband that very evening.

While Masih was asleep inside Baba's house, about three hundred yards away, Aziz, Jawad, Khalifa, Baba, Sori, and Mulla Salim gathered around Nadia and the empty grave. They had decided to keep only one lantern dimly lit to avoid attracting villagers' attention. Although, at that time of the night, everyone stayed indoors, the participants knew that danger loomed heavily. Informants were everywhere, and it was best not to risk a surprise visit by a secret police vehicle or a Soviet gunship helicopter.

Nadia looked at the content of the wooden box under the faint light and planted a kiss on it. Then, she handed the case to Baba. He leaned down and, using both hands, passed it on to Aziz, who had already descended into the pit.

After everyone helped pour the soil in, Sekandar planted a green flag on the damp mound. As the wolves howled from faraway, Mulla Salim recited verses from the Holy Quran, prayed for the liberation of Afghanistan from the yoke of communism, and advised the survivors of the martyr to remember God and seek assistance from Him.

"My sister, your martyred husband is the pride of Deh Darya and the pride of Afghanistan," Salim said, standing in front of Nadia, with Dr. Sharif's grave in between. The frail flame of the kerosene lamp casted a long, flickering shadow on her grief-stricken face. He continued, "Let me humbly offer my condolences as well as congratulations to you. For your husband has achieved martyrdom, the greatest honor a man could ever attain. Accept God's will as we are all destined to return to Him."

She sobbed.

SEVENTEEN

Masih remembered Father saying, *you are supposed to read, not destroy them*, as he stood in the doorway, watching his son cut through the pages of his magazines with scissors. Although Father sounded serious, he was smiling.

He would cut those images and place them one by one into a black folder. The photos were of skyscrapers, historic architectural sites, and castles. Next to the stack of magazines, a yellow folder lay on the floor in which Masih kept dozens of his own sketches of various structures.

Often, following the Friday prayer, when Father came home from the mosque and leaned against a large pillow on his bed to read or listen to the radio, Masih would jump next to him and demand his undivided attention. He would show him his collection of photos and outlines. Father would put his reading aside, turn the volume of the radio down, and lend his eyes and ears to what interested Masih. He was glad that his son showed interest in architectural design from an early age.

He would assess each one of Masih's sketches, asking questions and sometimes offering a suggestion or two to improve the drawing, "Not bad. *Affarin*, bravo. You can be an architect. You have the talent, but you'll have to study hard to get there."

Hearing those remarks, Masih would smile and his face glow with pride. After all, Father was a *Kharej-rafta*, a man who had gone abroad; he had lived in America, and seen real skyscrapers. He definitely knew what a nice modern architectural piece looked like.

***

In a framed photo, sitting on the table next to Masih's bed, Father was wearing a diamond-shaped graduation cap, a shiny black gown, a white dress shirt, and sported a blue tie. In his mid to late twenties, he looked a lot like Masih with a scrawny face and a head full of black hair. Father beamed with pride, looking straight into the camera, as if at the time of taking the photo, he knew that one day his son would be staring at him.

What if the photograph, somehow, magically came to life and started speaking to him? Masih would then ask him where he had been and how could he find him. When was he going to come back? A photo coming to life would have to be a miracle. He remembered Father telling him that prophets like Muhammad, Eisa, and Musa had made miracles happen. Yes, his name was *Masih*, Christ, but he was no prophet and definitely not capable of producing any miracles.

***

"Masih," Nadia was standing in the dark hallway.

"Yes, Mother."

"Aren't you going to leave them outside?"

The pigeons were dozing off with sleepy eyes. They had another boring day in captivity ahead, to which they could not have looked forward at all. The sudden exchange of words between Nadia and Masih jolted them to their feet.

Masih had already promised her not to keep them in his room, especially at night. But after finishing dinner, he had picked them up from the hallway and brought them in to lighten the burden of guilt on his own shoulders due to his failure to feed them on time.

"I will take them out, but what if *Haft-Dam*, the Seven Lives gets a hold of them?" Masih said.

The cat seemed to be the subject of every conversation in the neighborhood. Women and children, who gathered in the bread bakery, told fascinating stories about Haft Dam. People brought their already prepared dough to the bakery, which housed a clay oven much bigger than the one Sori was using in the village.

Swearing that he had seen it in action with his own eyes, one of the boys in the bakery had said, "Haft Dam is so fast, he can leap and catch a flying bird."

An elderly woman had held up her hands toward the sky, asking God to destroy the cat that had stolen the beef that she had salted and secured in a cold room, "I remember shutting the door tight. That clever beast must have turned the door knob with his paws."

Yet, the customers at the bakery disagreed about his size and color. Some claimed with certainty that the animal was in fact as fat and big as a bear. They believed that the creature's black, velvety hair that shone under the sun and gleamed in the moonlight had covered multiple layers of fat around his giant frame. He mustered a hypnotic power in his glossy green eyes that paralyzed his prey. And if anyone tried to chase or throw stones at him, at first, he would run, but then he would surprise his hunter with a quick turnaround and charge at full speed. At that point, if not hypnotized, the pursuer must either escape or prepare for a painful death.

Others argued that Haft Dam didn't even come close to being stocky. A lean body, long legs, and pointy ears made him look more like a panther then a bear. In fact, he might as well have been a panther.

"I have never heard him meow," said one of the boys who supported the panther theory.

It was not clear how much of what people were saying about the Seven Lives was true and how much was the product of their imagination. However, in the midst of that mingled heap of fact and fiction, no one doubted that the ubiquitous cat was indeed incredibly strong, agile, and cunning, with razor-sharp teeth and paws as strong as those of a lion. *Peshak* or *palang*, cat or tiger, whatever it was, the neighborhood seemed to be terrified by it, and now that people were aware of Haft Dam's abilities, they became extra protective of their belongings that could have meant food for the animal. Therefore, lately, the beast must have been starving and determined to find a meal.

Masih placed the cage in the hallway against the wall. Then, he pushed the knob on the screen door a couple of times to make sure that it was locked. He left the main door slightly ajar. In that hot summer night, without electricity, keeping the door shut would have meant a restless night for everyone. Masih was certain that Haft Dam would not be able to enter the hallway by penetrating through a hole, tiny as the open end of a pencil sharpener, in the screen.

***

Father might return tomorrow, if not, some other day. Eventually, he'll come. The doorbell will ring; Masih will answer, and find him standing there. Masih closed his eyes and darkness prevailed.

***

The leading tank of the convoy idled on the road by Habibia high school's gate, and the fleet extended toward the Darul-Aman Palace as far as the eye could see. Diesel fume and dust assaulted Masih's nostrils and lungs. Wearing a green military helmet, Bital had pulled his torso out from the roof of the leading tank. Soviet soldiers peeked out of the other vehicles behind him. Then, he flung his fist up and shouted as loud as he could, "Hoorah! Hoorah!" The Soviets too punched the air, "Hoorah! Hoorah! Hoorah!" Their faces blazed with hatred, their eyes widened with rage. Those furious cries revealed their glistening front teeth, sharp as those of a wolf.

"Comrade Masih," from atop the tank, Bital summoned him with a violent hand gesture.

Masih stepped forward and away from the school gate without any objection, without even thinking.

"Let's go and destroy the enemies of the revolution," Bital said, inviting him to climb up the giant vehicle.

"No!"

Masih turned. It was Father, shouting from behind the iron gate. He had lost a lot of weight and looked terrified. Dark circles surrounded his eyes, "Don't son, don't go. You'll regret it." He clasped the iron rods of the gate with both hands.

Masih stared at Father, but showed no reaction, not a word, not even a blink, as if he couldn't recognize him anymore. Then, he dropped his books on the dusty sidewalk and leaped up on the tank.

"That way," Masih pointed with his index finger, "Deh Darya is over there."

***

The Soviets surrounded the village. Bital turned to Masih and shouted over the roar of the machines, "Where are those brothers?"

Pointing toward Baba Sekandar's house, Masih said, "Over there, the first house by the river."

The tank turned its barrel toward the mud-house and aimed. Aziz and Jawad were standing on the rooftop. Their eyes followed their flock of doves, flying in a circle above the house. They seemed to have no clue about the convoy's presence, about the tank aiming at their house, only a few yards away across the graveyard.

"Ready?" Bital screamed, flashing his pointed fangs.

The Soviet operator nodded with a smirk.

"Fire!" his voice bounced off the mountains.

"Wait, don't," Masih tried to scream, but choked. His lips locked. The roar of the cannon rattled the mountains.

It was too late.

***

As though the bullet had hit him in the back, Masih catapulted forward, sat upright, feeling the choke in his throat. He still wanted to scream, but couldn't. Then he looked around. There were no tanks, no Bital, no Deh Darya. It was just another bad dream. At last, amidst the humidity and heat, he was able to take a breath.

The moon, like an enormous silver coin had cast a thin glow over the gloom of the night. Masih's shirt was sticking to his skin. Sweat streamed off his temples and ran down his neck. He took a few more breaths, thanking God that he awoke, and the nightmare was over.

But within a few seconds, a distinct sound of metal, scraping against the cemented surface of the hallway, interrupted his thoughts.

EIGHTEEN

Was this the beginning of another nightmare? Unsure, Masih stood up and flipped the light switch, but the room stayed dark. Only a pale moonlight shimmered through the open window. It must have been past ten o'clock, as electricity cut off around that time almost every night.

What was that scratching sound about? Was Mother okay? He jumped out of the room without bothering to light the candle, which he always kept next to Father's framed photo.

But as soon as he hurried into the hallway, he realized what had happened. The cage had disappeared. In an instant, his heart began thumping again. He bent down and examined the floor, hoping to find it in a corner of the hallway. Dispersed white feathers wandered under a faint gleam of the moonlight.

Haft Dam! Although he had never seen the beast, the image of a panther flashed in his mind. How was it possible that he had opened a locked door? Then, he heard another sound from around the corner, further down the hall. He sprinted toward the source and turned to face the screen door, which he had locked earlier that night. There it was, the cage, bumped and beaten, lying next to the battered screen door—the birds still inside. Mother sat next to it, hugging her knees and shaking her head with sorrow and regret.

Terrified, the doves flapped their wings in vain. Sheer horror was the only image reflecting in their eyes' tiny mirrors. They knew that they had just fallen short of becoming the big cat's meal. Apparently, they were still not sure the danger had passed, their little hearts kept racing, fearful of whatever might happen next.

The small hole in the screen door had turned into a giant opening, torn in many directions. A big cat like Haft Dam could easily leap through it. Masih stepped outside on the terrace. He looked around. Crickets chirped nonstop, but it seemed every other living creature on earth remained still and silent. There was no trace of the predator anywhere. As it had heard Mother's footsteps, it must have dashed and jumped up on a roof or scaled a wall with a single bound. With God's blessing, he had not been able to open the cage. The situation could have been much worse. Masih would have had to live the rest of his life with the guilt of being responsible, or at least partially responsible for the brutal murder of his doves.

"You have to let them free. It's a sin, you know," still sitting next to the cage, Mother said with an admonishing tone.

"I will," he answered without turning around. She was right. They needed to fly and live their lives like every other dove. They didn't deserve to live in a cage or a dove-house. It was about time for them to learn to be free. Had they not been captive, this would not have happened.

Barefoot, he stood there, thinking about how wrong it was to keep two innocent pigeons imprisoned for no reason. He had done exactly what the government had done to his father. This time, Haft Dam failed, but it would definitely try again. Masih could not turn and look at the doves or Mother straight in the eye. He kept staring at the dark shadows of trees around the courtyard. They had nothing to say. There was nothing to say. Masih knew exactly what he was going to do at dawn.

***

At sunrise, Nadia was sitting on her bed, with books and scrap papers scattered all around her. Colored pastels, pencils, magazines, scissors, and a cup filled with glue were among the tools with which she prepared her teaching material for the upcoming week. A cardboard box, packed with more magazines, pastels, and papers sat on the carpeted floor. Assigned to teach second graders, she was hard at work cutting, drawing, and writing words with big letters.

She had also placed an English dictionary, a book about English grammar, and a spiral notebook on her side. Her plan was to complete the teaching project, then study English. She had begun learning the language in sixth grade. Thereafter, throughout her school years at Rabea-e Balkhi high school as well as in Kabul University, she had continued to self-study the foreign language that was supposed to be the key to success.

It's the international language. If you learn it, you'll qualify for so many jobs anywhere in the world, Sharif used to say.

***

Nadia could hear the shuffle of her son's footsteps through the hallway. Looking up, she found him standing by her bedroom door. The damaged cage dangled from his right hand. He glanced at it and said with a sad tone, "I am letting them go."

"Bravo! That's the right thing to do."

In the courtyard, he placed the cage by the wall, on the cemented path, and looked up. The sky was as blue as he had ever seen. The sun, which had risen not too long ago, hurled a blinding arrow at his eyes. It was a perfect day for his birds to fly and experience freedom.

Masih opened the tiny door of the cage. Then, he stepped back and leaned against the wall.

The doves didn't make a move, as though they couldn't believe their eyes. Maybe, they were so used to captivity that they didn't want to leave. Maybe they thought Haft Dam was still out there waiting for them to come out.

After a minute or two, one of them turned toward the open gate and jumped out on the cemented path. The other simply followed, emulating the act. They took a few steps turning to the left and to the right. Then, as Masih's eyes followed them, they flapped their wings, flew to the edge of the rooftop, and sat side by side.

What were they waiting for? Certainly, they hadn't forgotten how to fly. So, what was the problem? Maybe they were afraid to be free, just as Aziz and Jawad had guessed. Even if they did fly, they had nowhere to go.

Once again, the sun assaulted his eyes. He closed them and looked down for a few seconds to ease the pain. As he raised his gaze, he saw another dove, a third dove circling around in the silky blue sky right above the house.

Each circle was an invitation for the newly liberated doves to join him. They responded by stepping from side to side, seemingly eager. They had to make a decision whether to fly or to stay put.

Masih thought of whistling to encourage the birds to join the newcomer that could guide them back to the free world. He brought his hand to his mouth but stopped short of finishing the act. Maybe, they simply didn't want to leave. And if they did fly away, it had to be their decision.

At last, seconds after the third dove headed for the Asmayee Mountain, Masih's guests made their decision; they fluttered their wings and accepted the invitation. Flying behind the third dove, they traveled farther and higher, and within a few seconds, all three disappeared into the embrace of the mountain.

"Like us, they have the right to be free. I am sure they are thankful to you," standing next to the battered screen door, Mother said, "now, let's fix this door before Haft Dam comes after you and me."

"Good idea," he said, forcing a smile.

***

Located on the fourth floor of the building, the library of Habibia high school was spacious. As Masih entered the room, he noticed Bital, sitting behind a desk in the center of a stage-like structure on the right-hand side. About three dozen chairs, facing the stage, filled the space between the elevated structure and the bookshelves toward the rear end of the room. Although members of the Youth Organization occupied most of the seats, for a school with some three thousand students, the number of boys attending the meeting did not seem particularly impressive.

On the left side, by the window a giant globe stood on a stand, next to which on a tall table, a large book was left open. It seemed to be thousands of pages thick and filled with tiny writings, colored images, and illustrations. When making a trip with Father to the main public library a long time ago, Masih had learned that this kind of book was different from all other books. It was called an encyclopedia, containing information about anything and everything.

Masih walked past the globe and the book of all books, and chose one of the few empty chairs in the last row by the dusty bookshelves. He tried to conceal his nervousness and not show any signs of worry or guilt that needled his thoughts. That was the first time he had participated in a meeting of the Youth Organization, which officially made him a communist, and a traitor—in exchange for a piece of paper. Masih had cowardly auctioned his soul so he could keep his body alive. He had never been as disappointed in himself as when he stepped into that meeting.

"Comrades," clearing his throat, Bital said aloud to attract the attention of the participants, "Let's begin the very first general meeting of the year, shall we?" his commanding voice spread an utter silence around the room, with all eyes fixed on him.

"First, let me introduce three of our comrades who have joined us recently."

This moment of introduction was what Masih dreaded all week long. Bital had specifically asked Masih to attend the meeting so he could formally introduce him to other members of the organization. He introduced two other boys who seemed a year or two older than Masih. Keeping their head up, they walked toward the stage and received their red membership card from Bital. With a brief applause, the existing members expressed their recognition of the *morgha-e naw*, the new birds.

Then Bital announced Masih's name, glancing toward him with a smile. A few of the boys turned and looked at Masih. With a pounding heart, sweaty palms, and a gaze fixed on the floor, it took him a long time to reach the stage.

Masih Sharif was now officially a *rafiq*, a comrade. Could there be a *be-ghairati*, dishonorable act greater than that? He couldn't think of one. It wouldn't be too long before his classmates and other kids in school found out that he too had become a Marxist, and one could not be a Marxist and a Muslim at the same time. They will no longer speak to or even greet him. In fact, they will make his life miserable with all kinds of taunts and insults. Nobody likes a *sazmani*, a member of the organization, and nobody would want to be friends with one.

With a trembling hand, he received his already laminated, red membership card.

"Comrades, today I want to talk about a few issues, and I want to be frank," Bital said.

Everyone stopped their chitchat, straightened up, and focused on Bital.

He continued, "We should make people understand that our revolution is a peoples' revolution. It is a progressive surge against which no element, be it an individual, an organization, or a country can resist. For us, a return to the feudalist era of the past is not an option. No one can defeat this movement, neither the American imperialists nor their Arab and Pakistani slaves."

For a few seconds, Bital glanced at a paper lying on the table in front of him. Then he went on, "Unfortunately, our deceived brothers are fighting against the interests of their own country in the name of *jihad*. The enemy is desperately trying to trap youths just like you in their maze of propaganda. Beware not to be fooled. They are nothing but slaves of the world-gobbling American imperialism." He pounded his fist on the desk and paused, waiting for his comrades to applaud.

Following the brief ovation, Bital went on, "The second point I would like to make is that the friendly Soviet forces have come here to help us. They are creating the necessary conditions for progress, for ending misery and poverty in Afghanistan. They defend our country against the American, Pakistani, Chinese, and Iranian invaders. But remember, if we Afghans don't fight for our own country, no foreigner will ever protect Afghanistan. We have to take our destiny into our own hand. Comrades, you should make every effort to enlighten people, be it your friends, family, or neighbors. Always try to convince them that our path is the only path that will lead to victory and prosperity. And if some prove too difficult to convince, then talk to me about them."

Talk to me about them? What does that mean? Play a snitch and betray your own family members, so you can send them to jail? How shameless! Masih could have easily contested every one of Bital's arguments. What he had just called a revolution was in fact a coup, executed by a handful of military officers. Second, an invading and occupying force could never defend the liberty of Afghanistan. If the goal of this government was to make people happy, then why did it throw thousands of innocent people in jail? For example, what was Father's fault? Why did it rob Mother of her happiness?

His desire to stand up and voice his opinions grew stronger by the second. But, it was obvious that the slightest protest, complaint, or unfavorable reaction would expel him from school and even land him into jail. Then what would happen to Mother, losing both her husband and son?

He had seen her many times with teary eyes, flipping through her wedding photo album. Masih didn't know how to help Mother stop being depressed. He didn't know if it was possible for her to be happy at all. However, what he did know was that he must never cause her any grief. His open opposition to Bital's claims would get him in trouble, and sadden her even more.

***

As the meeting was adjourned, according to Bital's order, the attendees divided into groups of four to seven members.

Bahram, Masih's group leader spoke about the importance of reporting the activities of *Ashrar*, thugs either to the meeting or directly to Bital himself. He said that pointing them out to the authorities was the moral duty of any comrade, "This way you can prevent the thugs from killing innocent people."

In response to Bahram's question as to whether anyone wanted to present a report, one of the boys said, "I actually have a report."

"Comrade Hamid, please share it with us," said Bahram.

"One of the boys in our neighborhood brought out a gun from his house."

Masih shuddered at the thought that some other boy like this idiot might have given a false report about Father too. Father had committed no crime. His fault was that he could not keep his opinions about the government to himself, and that he cared about Afghanistan. Father had not been involved with the *mujahedin*. Masih was certain of that. Every morning, he left home for his tiny clinic in Kot-e Sangi and returned sometime between five and six o'clock in the afternoon. He was a good man who took care of his family and his patients. That was all he did. Who knows? Maybe one of his patients had given the government a false report. It all must have been a big mistake.

***

"Did he say where he kept the gun?" Bahram asked. Rumors had it that Bahram was a third-degree black belt in Tae Kwon Do, a sport almost as popular as soccer among the boys in Kabul. However, as a gesture of modesty, He had repeatedly denied having anything to do with martial arts. Although he spoke softly and smiled at everyone, kids believed he was a dangerous fighter.

"No, I didn't ask. I figured it would sound too obvious. I didn't want him to think that I was up to something. He showed us one other thing, a piece of shrapnel too. He said he had brought it from a village in Logar province."

Bahram's green eyes, which made Masih think of Aziz, glittered. "Where in Logar?"

"I don't know, some village."

"What's this boy's name?"

"I don't know him well. I think his name is Ali.

Bahram didn't seem satisfied with his answer. In fact, he clearly seemed vexed by the immaturity with which comrade Hamid had handled this seemingly simple, and yet important case.

"Look," he leaned forward, placing his elbows on his short, chunky thighs, "it doesn't work like this. You should first find out what his name is, where he lives, what his Dad does for a living, and who gave him the pistol? You are missing a lot of information about this guy."

If the secret police began to pursue this boy's case, they will eventually raid his house and arrest him and his father, and they will take them to a place where no one could find them. Following Father' arrest, Masih and Nadia had gone to Pul-e Charkhi prison, the Interior Ministry, and about a thousand KhAD offices around the city to find him. Every one of the government officers, whom they had spoken to, acted as if they had never heard about the detainee. They pretended as if they wanted to help, but never did.

"By God sister," they swore as if they believed in God, "at this office we have no information about your husband."

A few of them even had the audacity to ask, "Are you sure the government officers arrested your husband? This government would never do such a thing." They would shamelessly lie and claim ignorance.

***

"I think his uncle is a *mujahed*," comrade Hamid said hesitantly.

"A *mujahed* is someone who fights for truth. You mean *Ashrar*, thugs?" Bahram failed to hide the fury resounding in his voice.

In an instant, Hamid's cheeks turned red, "Yes, I mean *Ashrar*," he said without looking at Bahram's piercing eyes.

"You see, it is things like this that bother me the most. If you and I call the enemies of our nation *mujahed*, then what can we expect the villagers to call them?" Masih was waiting to see him deliver a sidekick, Bruce Lee style, to Hamid's chubby face. Instead, Bahram said, "Comrade thanks for the report. It's good. It's a good start. But it's not enough. You should work on this case some more. Let's talk to comrade Samad about it. He can introduce you to someone from the *Khadamat* 'services' in charge of your district."

Then, with a serious expression that formed creases across Bahram's forehead, he addressed the group, "It's extremely important that we keep our eyes and ears open. We must disclose the evil deeds of the enemy." Without making an effort to turn his head around, he rotated his eyeballs, meeting each comrade's eyes individually to ensure everyone understood what he meant.

"Does anyone else have anything to share?" he asked, expecting to hear at least a couple of positive responses.

No one seemed to have the answer he was looking for. Perhaps, the reason they didn't have a report was that they too were forced to join the organization.

"Okay, so nobody has a report and no attempts at recruiting new members?" he seemed disappointed. "In that case, our meeting is adjourned."

That was the best news Masih had heard that day.

***

"Listen up," Bital stood and hollered amidst the chatter of the participants. Immediately, everyone stopped talking and faced the stage where he stood with his hands held up as if to gesture his surrender. "Those comrades interested in practicing soccer meet me in the fields under the maple trees in ten minutes." He had promised to show a few cool tricks to those who attended the general meeting. Most of the members began to gather around Bital, determined to follow him to the soccer field. If Masih were ever to learn soccer, this was his opportunity. Of all the boys present in that room, he was probably the one who needed coaching the most. He was in great need of learning, for example, how to stop and keep the ball from bouncing on its own; or, how to kick it so it rolls where he wants it and not wherever it wants to roll. The opportunity had presented itself for Masih to find a solution to these and many other problems that kept him on the sidelines during every match. Also, if he became a good soccer player, Father would be proud of him—once he returns.

Dr. Sharif was well aware that his son loved to play soccer but did not play well. He had hoped that perhaps just by watching the games, he would pick up some skills. So he would take him to Kabul's only stadium to watch matches between Afghanistan and countries like Iran, India, and Uzbekistan. Sharif had also tried to teach him a trick or two in their backyard.

"Don't get nervous; just keep your eyes up," he would advise.

Judging by the manner in which Father controlled the ball, and some amazing stories Masih had heard from him about his soccer playing days when he was a student at Ahmad Shah Baba high school in Kandahar, he must have been a star athlete back then.

Now, training with Samad-e Bital seemed appealing. A quick transformation would certainly make Father proud. Like Father, perhaps Masih too could become a great soccer player.

But as tempting as the prospect of attending the training session was, he didn't follow Bital to the field. When it came to joining the soccer training camp, Masih *did* have a choice. He decided not to follow the footsteps of a man who was, according to Mulla Salim, a *Kafer,* infidel, selling out his religion and country to the Soviets. Men like him were directly responsible for the disappearance of Father.

NINETEEN

It took Masih only seconds to hurry out into the hallway. If the sky turned dark prior to his arrival, Mother would be pacing back and forth by the front door.

"Comrade Masih, *peroz bashi*, be victorious," standing next to the stairs, Bital smiled. He was waiting for the rest of his trainees to join him.

Be victorious? What happened to saying *Khoda hafez*, in God's protection? Then again, why expect Bital to say something like that? Those who say, in God's protection, actually believe in God.

Masih did not respond as he dashed down the stairs.

***

"You are late. Where were you?" those were the exact words he had expected to hear from Mother.

"There was a soccer match at school. Sorry, I lost track of time watching it," he said, avoiding her gaze.

How could he disclose the truth? How could he tell her that her son had just returned from a meeting with the same people who had kidnapped her husband? Yes, Masih had lied to Mother, but he had no other choice. Telling her the truth would drag her deeper into the gloom. He had made a promise to Father to take care of her. No, he was not going to create more agony and heartache for her. No, she didn't deserve, nor could she endure any more distress. At any cost, he must avoid adding to her sorrows, even if he had to lie to her.

Maybe someday, once Father returns, he could explain the whole situation to both of them. Only then could he tell them why he had joined the Youth Organization, just the way he had justified it to himself. Now, however, was not the time.

"It's dark out there. It's not safe. You know *talashi*, the search force is everywhere."

"I know, I know Mother, sorry," he said reaching for a glass of water.

"Right after you finish eating," her voice softened, "you must study. First, you were wasting time with those doves; now you're keeping busy watching soccer. You'll have to take responsibility for the entrance exam. It is around the corner. You have to start preparing for it early."

"What are you talking about? I have three years to study."

Nadia entered the kitchen, walked toward him, and looked him straight in the eyes. "The earlier you begin, the easier it gets. You must focus. You must plan early," she said with a commanding tone to convey absolute inflexibility.

***

Masih sat on his bed, scanning about a dozen photos that he had pinned and scotch-taped on the opposite wall. Skyscrapers glistened, towering over the major developed cities of the world: New York, Tokyo, Chicago, Toronto, Paris, Hong Kong, Singapore, and a few others. Of course, Kabul was not among them, simply because there were no skyscrapers in Kabul. The tallest structure in downtown was the Fourteen-Flight-Building.

He looked at the image of a building he had sketched a year ago. *Not a bad draft, if I say so myself.* He smiled. Would he ever learn to design an actual building?

Some of the best universities are in America. If you study hard, you could get a scholarship and study there as I did. Father used to say. Will he ever come back? How soon? Tomorrow? A year from now? Five years? If Masih could help the *mujahedin* topple the government and expel Soviets from Afghanistan, Father will come back much sooner. *Don't worry, one day I will be a mujahed. I'll bring you home.* He glanced at father's beaming photo, blew off the candle, pulled the blanket over, and closed his eyes. Father kept smiling.

***

A week later, one afternoon Masih leaned against the front door, facing the crowded main street. Carts, cars, buses, motorcycles, and donkey-led carriages shared the road.

He observed some pedestrians wearing traditional clothes while others strolled with Western-style garments on the busy sidewalk. After Father's arrest, he would often find himself standing at the same spot, watching the crowd pass by—hoping to be surprised, hoping for a miracle to happen. Father could suddenly appear among the crowd, from nowhere! After such a long time, a hug would be nice. Masih would hold on to him and never let go. One day, he *will* be surprised. It could be today or some other day. He *will* see Father again. He was sure of that. Eventually, the Marxists will recognize that they had made a terrible mistake, that they had jailed an innocent man. Then, they will apologize to and set him free. *God is kind. Never lose hope, son.* Father said, every time the Afghans lost to a foreign team.

***

Four high school girls, wearing navy-blue uniforms, strolled by. They seemed to be in no particular rush. White scarves hung loosely around their shoulders, and only a thin layer of black nylon covered their shapely calves. Sori would never be allowed to expose her legs like that in public, none of the girls in the villages did. While passing by, they looked up and pretended not to have noticed him standing only a couple of feet away. A few steps farther, the one on the left looked back only to catch Masih's eyes glued to her calves. Her smile said a lot. She didn't mind the stare, and her brown eyes and dark eyelashes gave Masih a taste of how Noor must have felt during his little flirting episode with Sori.

There were quite a few schoolgirls around town, most of whom wore various amounts of make-up to enhance their good looks. None, however, could match Sori's natural beauty.

***

"Salam Masih," the voice from under a blue *chadari*, veil belonged to Sori. Surprised, Masih was sure of it. Still, he couldn't believe that Sori was standing in front of him. She never travelled to Kabul all by herself. Either Baba or one of the boys would accompany her when coming to the city.

"Salam Sori?" he said without trying to hide his astonishment.

"It's me, Sori," she placed a cloth package on the ground to free her hands and lift the front edge of her veil, revealing her teary, sleepless eyes.

"Is everything okay? Where is Baba?"

"I will . . . I'll tell you later. Baba . . ." her throat chocking, she was unable to finish her sentence.

Masih was anxious to know what happened. But he didn't ask. Sori was trembling, and seemingly about to collapse. He picked up the package and led the way inside.

***

Lifting her eyes from her book, Nadia saw what she had feared and anticipated all along since her return from Deh Darya. As Sori entered the room, she stood up and rushed toward her. Embracing the girl she had raised as her own daughter, Nadia could feel Sori's warm tears soaking her shoulder. The women held on to each other without saying a word.

At last, Sori broke the silence with a plea, "Mother, please don't let him marry me off to that robber."

"After any darkness, there is light. God is kind," looking at her directly in the eyes, she clasped her arms to straighten her up.

***

The sun had just left for the other side of the earth, and it was dark enough to light the candles. The clock on the wall showed eleven past eight. Five or six nights a week, utter darkness loomed around the neighborhood, thanks to the antigovernment forces for destroying the power lines. Masih sat on the mattress across from Sori and listened. She spoke of how much she hated Sarwar and how unfair it was of Baba to have given her *lafz*, a promise of engagement to Qayoum Khan without her consent or even knowledge.

Occasionally, she wiped her tears and nose with a damp embroidered handkerchief crumpled in between her slender fingers.

"I would rather die than to marry a man like him. He has no manners, no values, and no education whatsoever," Sori said, adding to a string of other unfavorable descriptions of Sarwar that she had listed since her arrival. It puzzled Masih. How could a bad person like Sarwar be a *mujahed* commander and deserve a wife like Sori?

133

"My future is already destroyed by that bulldog," Sori's comment broke Masih's train of thoughts, "first he torched my school; now he wants to make my life even more miserable until I die. If I marry him, he will take me to Pakistan. He will force me to do nothing but cook and clean for him and his men. God knows when I will ever see Deh Darya again. Both my school and my dreams are already lying in ashes."

Although, Sori said nothing about Noor, to Masih it was obvious her heart ached for him. He searched for words to form a sentence, any sentence to soothe Sori's pain. But as he was thinking to conjure up some positive statement, Mother came to his rescue, "My daughter, don't lose heart. I'll talk to your father. God willing, he will change his mind." She sat next to Sori and gently touched her curly hair. Then, to change the subject, she turned to Masih, "Tell her the story of your doves. Tell her what happened."

"What happened? Nothing happened," he said defensively, "I just . . . let them go."

"Come on, you are already forgetting all the details? Tell Sori about what Haft Dam did."

"Mother, there are no details." Why would she want Sori to find out how incapable he was of taking care of a couple of birds? The whole story was pointless and embarrassing. Sometimes he just didn't understand Mother.

Sori said, "You did a good thing. I keep asking my brothers to let their birds free, but they always make excuses. They blame the pigeons for wanting to return every time they send them out."

Mother said, "Your sister has been upset all day long. Come on, can you help change the subject?"

Sister? The fact that Sori had spent the first six years of her life at their house or the fact that both had been breastfed by Mother didn't make her exactly his sister. But that was not how Mother saw it. She said that they were *shiri*, milk siblings. Masih, however, didn't even remember spending a day with Sori under the same roof, or Sori being fed his mother's milk.

Nevertheless, Mother was right. The only way to stop Sori from weeping was to divert her attention from her predicament on a different issue. Somehow the crying had to stop, and if that meant embarrassment on his part, then so be it.

"Okay, I will tell her the story," he said sitting upright, "but I hope you understand it wasn't my fault."

"What wasn't your fault?" Sori asked.

"Well, they kind'a got in trouble."

"How?" she seemed genuinely interested.

Masih told her the whole story, explaining every detail about Haft Dam's attempt at his birds' life, from the time he had heard the sound of metal dragging against the floor, until the birds flew away behind the Asmayee Mountain, "suddenly, a third dove showed up from nowhere. It was a *Kaghazi*, Paper White, just like the other two. He kept flying around the house," He circled his index finger pointing toward the ceiling, "finally, my doves joined him. They flew higher and higher and disappeared behind the mountains."

"Maybe God had sent him to guide your doves. They are little angels on earth, you know. Nobody should keep any bird in a cage. I think all creatures have the right to live free."

Masih smiled, knowing that Sori had calmed and that she too had approved of what he had done. "I wish I had let them free from the beginning, though. They wouldn't have had to go through that horrible experience."

"Well, you let them free at the right time. The weather is warm, and with the third dove's help, they'll survive."

He shook his head in agreement, remembering how suffocated he felt while sitting in the back of that military truck and in the meeting at the school library. Thank God, Mother had already told her about his little adventure on their way back from Deh Darya.

***

The clock indicated fifteen minutes past nine. Masih should have gone to bed if he were to not fall asleep in the classroom tomorrow. But, he was awake as an owl, still sitting on a mattress across from Sori.

For sure, Baba Sekandar will arrive, looking for his daughter, any time. He would grab Sori's wrist and drag her back to Deh Darya. Then immediately, he would send one of his sons after Mulla Salim and Sarwar to conduct the *nekah*, the legal marriage ceremony. Sori would have no choice but to mutter a 'yes' to the Mulla's question. *Do you accept this man, Qomandan Muhammad Sarwar, the son of Muhammad Qayoum Khan in your Aqd-e Nekah, contract of marriage?*

Sori's bloodshot eyes looked as puffy as Masih had seen them earlier that afternoon. Cup after cup, green tea had turned into endless streams of tears, rolling down her colorless face. She continued to clench the handkerchief, with which she would periodically wipe her eyes and nose.

***

Masih and Mother were startled when they heard someone pounding on the metal gate. Sori leapt off the mattress to the center of the room, letting the hot cup of tea fly from her shaking hands and land on her lap. She shrieked, not because the hot liquid had burned her thigh, but because she knew who was on the other side of the front door.

Masih jumped out of the room and dashed toward the gate. The pounding continued, even louder than the first time. Following her son, Nadia rushed out too.

"Who is it?" Masih shouted.

"Is she there?" yelling from behind the gate, the voice was that of Sekandar's. Masih had guessed right that Baba would eventually show up.

"Baba, calm down, she is here," Nadia said, as she marched behind Masih.

"I'm not going to let her live. She has dishonored me. My own daughter, my own blood," anger shook his voice.

***

That morning, when Sori had prepared tea and served it to her father with *noql*, sugar coated almonds, Baba had asked her to sit down because he had something important to tell her. He told her that he would have to give a positive response to Sarwar's request for her hand. Before his refusal to give his daughter's hand to Daoud from Deh Bala, he didn't bother to speak with her. This time, however, despite the fact that he had correctly predicted her reaction, he had decided to raise the issue so he could tell her about his decision.

Sekandar also feared that a fight with his educated daughter was bound to break out. Nevertheless, eventually, he had to inform her of his verdict before sharing it with her brothers and Sarwar's family. For days on end, Baba had brainstormed, looking for reasons to convince Sori that marrying Sarwar was not such a bad idea. He would have to highlight some good qualities of Sarwar's character—not an easy task to accomplish.

About as tall as Sekandar himself, Sarwar was the son of a man who ruled the village, of course with support from Mulla Salim and elders like Sekandar. He had worked very little, that is, if bossing around men who worked for his father is to be considered a job. About a year before the communist coup, the twenty-year-old worked in his father's wholesale store in Mandawi market for about two weeks. But his *chaqo kashi*, knife-drawing incident with the porter ended what his father hoped to be the beginning of a successful business career for him.

***

One day, the porter complained about a stabbing pain in his lower back that prevented him from shouldering a sack of grains up the final four steps and into the store. For this reason, Sarwar decided to pay him only half of the amount originally agreed upon. Feeling disgraced by the manner in which Sarwar spoke to him, the laborer refused to accept his unfair offer and insisted on being paid the full amount.

Sarwar pushed him out of the store and pointed to the undelivered sack, "You will get your money when I see it delivered *inside* the shop."

The porter did not appreciate his rude tone and rough treatment. He forgot all about the throbbing pain and charged at full speed. In no time, he lifted Sarwar and tossed him on sacks of flour piled in a corner. As he turned around to exit the store, the staggering, furious boy jumped back to his feet, thrusting the tip of a *qama*, a dagger that he had secured in a holster slightly above his right hip, into the man's shoulder blade. This was to make up for the embarrassing moment of being tossed away by a much older and smaller man, as other shopkeepers and customers watched.

Shocked and angered, the spectators rushed to the porter's aid. If Sarwar had any *ghairat*, honor, he would not have drawn a knife and attacked an unarmed man from behind. Whatever happened to those days when men fought like men? The shopkeepers who knew Sarwar over the years were disgusted but not surprised.

"*Na-mard*, coward," someone yelled from among the crowd gathering around the wounded man, "he did not pull a knife on you.

You should have fought him with bare hands, face to face—like a man."

"He is right. That's *be-ghairati*, a dishonorable act," others agreed as they helped the bleeding porter to a donkey-drawn carriage. They transported him to the hospital. Meanwhile, someone from among the crowd ran to the police station and reported the incident.

***

At the station, Qayoum Khan reached for his wallet and made an offer to the police chief, stating that he was willing to pay "the fine" for the "mistake" that his son had made.

"There is no need for this case to go to the court. My son is young and stupid. I ask you to forgive him."

Accepting all five of the crisp hundred Afghani bills, the chief agreed to release him.

Fired by his father, Sarwar would spend his summer days gambling, smoking *chars,* hashish, or chasing after high school girls in Kabul. In winters, he would bid on dogfights around the city. No one dared to inform Qayoum Khan about his son's habits. Sarwar would find the snitch and undoubtedly stab him with the same dagger that had sent the porter to the hospital.

***

Sekandar understood that it would be difficult to convince his daughter to marry Sarwar. Sori just wouldn't understand that no matter what, Sarwar was a *mujahedin* commander, willing to sacrifice his life for the freedom of Afghanistan and for Islam. Yes, he isn't perfect, but as time passed, he would mature, and the experience of *jihad* would teach him humility. In addition, marriage itself will teach him responsibility, Baba hoped.

On his journey to Kabul, all he thought about was offering these reasons to Sori. But none had sounded convincing enough, not even to himself. He knew Sarwar, and he knew his daughter well. Inheriting her mother's smarts and stubbornness, she would not be easily convinced. He had no idea what to do. What he did know was that he must bring his daughter home. If the villagers discovered that she had escaped to Kabul, Baba and his sons would be disgraced for the rest of their lives. How could a father let his daughter, his *namoos,* honor run away to the city? What will people say? They will say that she eloped with a *londa,* lover.

And what would Sekandar say to Qayoum Khan, to a man who was always there for him in times of adversity? If the villagers discovered that Sori had left home without her father's permission, then neither Sarwar nor anybody else would want to marry her. She was too young to realize that her life will be ruined.

"We are leaving right now," Baba said, standing in the doorway. The somber sound of his voice added to the necessary gravity for communicating the resolve with which he had come to take his daughter home. The expression on his aged face seemed calm, but a combination of fury and pain simmered in both chambers of his eyes.

Sori backed into the corner until her shoulder blades slammed against the wall, "Mother, don't let him take me. He's going to surrender me to that wolf," she pleaded to Nadia.

"*Dokhtarem*, my daughter, who am I to stop him? What kind of right have I earned to say anything?" It was impossible to ignore the sarcasm in her tone. Like a shield, she stood in the middle of the room between Sekandar and Sori.

Standing next to Baba, Masih looked up to witness his response. It seemed as if snow had fallen all over his head and face. Almost every single hair of his beard, the hair protruding from under his white turban, and even his eyebrows had turned white.

"Nadia, don't say that. You are like her mother. You have to make her understand. Otherwise, I will be disgraced. I will never be able to show my face to Qayoum Khan or to anybody in the village," Sekandar said while entering the room. Sori jolted back.

"You are telling me that I am her *mother*? All this time that they were proposing, you didn't even ask for my opinion. Now you are asking *me* to make her understand?" Pointing at Sori without looking at her, she said, "This girl is my daughter. I fed her my own milk. I spent six years raising her just the way Mahro would have done. Don't talk to me about honor. If anyone has become dishonored here, it is me."

"I told you, sister. You knew about everything, and you know about my situation too."

"I told you then, and I am telling you now. She should marry whomever *she* wants to marry."

Sori stood up and shouted, "Mother, you knew about this all along and never told me anything?"

"What was I going to tell you? That your father has decided to marry you to a man you hate?" she turned around, raising her hands, "I was against it from the beginning, but your father had already made up his mind."

"That man burned down my school. I'll never forgive him."

Baba stepped forward, "My daughter, Sarwar is not a bad man. This is wartime. In wars, these things happen."

"If he is a real man, why doesn't he go after the Soviets?" she asked with a coarse cry, "he is not a *mujahed*. He is a robber."

"Once he gets married, he will change. He will become a responsible, a better person."

"Baba, do you *really* believe that? Everybody knows who he is. You are so naive."

Nadia said, "This girl's life will be destroyed. Why don't you leave her with me? She was raised here. This is her house too. I will take care of her, I promise. Let her go to school here. She will become a great doctor one day."

"Sister, why don't you understand? She is not a little girl anymore. I can't leave my unwed daughter here in the middle of the city. What are people going to say? She is my *namoos,* honor. The only time a daughter leaves her father's house is when she gets married."

"Baba," Sori pleaded, "just tell Qayoum Khan that I refused. Please Baba, please!"

"Sori, if you don't marry this man, I will never be able to look Qayoum Khan in the eye. His wife wanted you for her son since I brought you back to—."

"So what?" Nadia jumped in, "just because they are wealthy, and their son is a commander, it doesn't mean they can buy any girl they want."

"Sister, what are you saying? Qayoum Khan is the King of the village. Yes, he can do whatever he wants. Plus, Qayoum Khan has done so much for me. Had he not given me that plot, where would I have raised my kids?"

"I don't care who he is. He is abusing his power, kidnapping your daughter and that's not right; that's against the law."

"Law? What law are you talking about? The laws of Kabul are only good for Kabul. Deh Darya has its own laws. The village is not like Kabul where fathers watch their daughters choose their husbands."

***

Years ago, Qayoum Khan had loaned Baba the money to cover his wedding expenses, and because Sekandar was a distant cousin, he had let him use his house for the ceremony. Qayoum Khan then went on to give him a plot of land as a wedding gift so Sekandar could build a house and raise his family in it. After the harvest season, he had ordered the men working for him to help Sekandar build the house before the arrival of winter. They finished construction in a couple of months. Then he moved his bride from a room in Qayoum Khan's compound to his newly built house. The Khan had also paid for Mahro's funeral, never asking for his money back. And when Sekandar was hospitalized in Aliabad hospital, Qayoum Khan had covered the expenses for his treatment. In addition, to honor his friend's hard work and loyalty, each year he would allocate a generous amount of corn and wheat for Sekandar regardless of the harvest's success.

Sekandar remembered everything his friend had done for him and was determined to pay him back with hard work and loyalty. It was true that he had worked on Qayoum Khan's land every year of his adult life, but so did many other men. In his mind, by working on his land and shop, supervising labor, and taking care of his livestock, Sekandar had fulfilled his duty as a loyal servant, nothing more. And that was the least he could do for a man who stood by him through thick and thin.

This was the first time that Qayoum Khan had asked Sekandar for a personal, real favor. And what he asked for did not require any special generosity or sacrifice. He had simply invited a man with no worldly means to be almost his equal. Establishing that sort of relationship with Qayoum Khan's family was the dream of many parents in Deh Darya and the surrounding villages.

If Sekandar failed to answer his friend's call, it would be a great embarrassment for Khan, and Sekandar would be viewed as an ungrateful man who doesn't value friendship. No doubt, the villagers will question his loyalty and honor. Who will trust him or his sons again? And in moments of hardship bound to come, there will be no one to call upon for help. If Sekandar failed, he would rather leave everything; abandon Deh Darya and never return.

***

Sori leaned back against the wall, closing her eyes and resting her forehead on her knees, "Khan shouldn't have helped you, expecting payback. He is using his power to force me into marrying his son. He might as well not have helped you at all. Why do *I* have to be punished?"

"Marrying him is not a punishment. In the beginning, it might be hard. But believe me, slowly Sarwar will change. You are a smart girl. You can change him," this time, Baba's tone had softened and the fire that blazed in his eyes moments ago subsided.

"I could never change him. Which of his habits would I change first? His gambling? His stealing? His dog fighting, knife fighting, which one? He carries a Kalashnikov on his shoulder and everybody calls him the commander. You tell me, how am I going to change him?"

Baba paused, and then did something that surprised everyone. As a pleading gesture, he kneeled, took his turban off, and placed it on the floor in front of Sori, "*Dokhtarem,* my daughter, I am begging you to say yes. I promise to talk to his father to change him. I will discuss all of your issues with him. Look, my *ezzat,* dignity is in your hands. I beg you my daughter; don't let me become dishonored at the end of my journey," he implored with a choking throat.

***

That night, Sori lay in the same corner that she was sitting all day long. Baba lay in the opposite corner, pulling a bedsheet over his head. She tried to shut her eyes, but a burning pain did not let her eyelids close. Soreness, the like of which she had never felt before, spread throughout her body. She looked out the window into the night. The moon had disappeared behind the clouds, and the stars had left the sky.

Where am I going to run from here? Is this it? Is this the end of the line?

The sound of Baba's snoring kept getting louder and louder. He must have been tired. He must have walked from downtown all the way to Kart-e Parwan. Baba hated those crowded busses that moved like ants, as he put it. *Walking would get you there a lot faster,* he used to say to Sori when they traveled to Kabul to shop and visit Dr. Sharif's family. They would stop by a Kabobi restaurant for a delicious serving of kabob or *mantu* dumplings followed by *falooda,* ice cream mixed with noodles and real snow from the mountains. On the way home, she would get to buy a flowery shirt or colorful glass bangles.

***

Despite his complaint about his everlasting back pain, Baba would let the seven-year-old Sori climb on his shoulders—she remembered. They would cross the bridge to the other side of the river, where the berry branches hung low and Sori could reach to handpick as many berries as she desired. Then, Baba would help her climb up a tree. Sori was the only girl in Deh Darya who climbed up the trees.

***

She was six-year-old when Baba brought her back from Kabul. Prior to her return, every Friday, Baba would come to the city to pray in Pul-e Kheshti, the central Mosque of the city, do some shopping, and most importantly visit his daughter in Dr. Sharif's house. He would buy sweets, sugarcoated almonds, and roasted nuts to offer to Sori. And as a gift, he would also bring a clay bowl of homemade yogurt, or a dozen eggs—his way of thanking Nadia and Dr. Sharif for raising his daughter.

During the Friday prayer, in the midst of Imam's recitation of sweet verses of the Holy Quran, another sweet sound would ring in Sekandar's ears, *Baba, Baba, Baba!* The melody of his daughter's voice that he was about to hear after an entire week.

On the final occasion when Sekandar had come to visit Sori, she had circled her tiny hands around Baba's neck and refused to say goodbye. When Baba explained to her that he had to get back to work the next day, she insisted on returning home with him.

That evening, Nadia, Dr. Sharif, and baby Masih accompanied Sori and Baba on his trip back to Deh Darya. The next day, Sharif's family returned to Kabul, but Sori decided to stay. Baba too had admitted that he could not let his daughter separate from him again. Throughout the day, she had followed him everywhere, climbed over his shoulders, said many new words and phrases, and played with his beard. For the first time since the death of his wife, happiness had returned to Baba's home. Afghans say *a woman is the light of the house.* He realized that his house was lit up for a second time.

Now, several years later, Sekandar had come to take Sori home again. This time, however, she would brighten someone else's home. This time, he would give Sori to a man whom she passionately disliked, and soon he will take her away to a strange land.

***

143

Baba had spent most days of his life, from dawn to dusk, laboring either on Qayoum Khan's land or in his store. Under decades of pressure and fatigue, he had permanently injured his spine. He did whatever he could to keep his children alive and raise them with dignity. He looked forward to seeing them eventually get married, and promote him from Baba to *Baba-kalan*, grandfather. He worked for Qayoum Khan but served his children—three precious gifts given to him by Mahro, a woman he loved and thought about every day of his life.

***

Since Sori was nine-years-old, she took care of Baba, washed his clothes, prepared his food, and poured water on his hands during ablution. *But all daughters are supposed to fulfill those duties, aren't they?* She thought. She had not done anything special for her father. Now, she had an opportunity to give him something in return. It was no longer possible to continue her studies and open the health clinic she had fancied. Now, her father's fate and honor were in her hands. He didn't deserve to be humiliated by his own daughter. Now it was Sori's duty to save Baba's honor. It would be her way of saying thank you to her father. After all, Sori's birth had led to the loss of the woman he loved. Staring at the starless sky, Sori made a decision.

***

The day following her return home, Baba confirmed that in a week, after the *Nekah*, marriage ceremony and wedding celebration, her husband would take her to a city called Quetta in Pakistan—a big city with many more people than Deh Darya.

"How long is he going to keep me there?" she asked with a quivering voice.

"I don't know, maybe until the *jihad* is over," Baba replied as if he was apologizing for making a terrible mistake.

"Will you come with me?"

"No my daughter, not right now, but once you are settled, I'll come and visit you," Baba said, running a trembling hand on her head.

***

About once or twice every three months, Sarwar traveled to Pakistan along with a few of his men to ensure that cash and weapons kept flowing in from the *Tanzim's*, organizations' headquarters. This was the order of things since about a year ago, and

Sarwar was getting agitated travelling back and forth mostly on foot. He had also grown tired of spending many days and nights in filthy guesthouses and eating spicy food that brought tears to his eyes. Even though he didn't mind losing money from gambling, he did not like wasting funds on lodging for a group of his starving men month after month.

Therefore, Sarwar rented a house in Quetta, big enough to host up to twenty men at a time. Now, he could take them to his own compound and have his wife cook for them.

***

Hearing the news from Baba, Sori nodded and said, "Okay." That was all she said; no objections or complaints, no questions asked. She had already decided to pay whatever the price to save Baba's *ezzat*, honor. If it meant marriage to Sarwar, and if it meant spending the rest of her life slaving for him, then so be it.

TWENTY

Kneeling down in the hallway, Masih spun his shoelaces between his fingers as fast as he could.

"Hurry, uncle is waiting for us," Mother called from the front yard. She could hear the diesel engine of the parked vehicle running. It was a special day, and Khalifa Zaman had decided not to make any rounds on the route. Instead, he would take his own and Dr. Sharif's family to Deh Darya.

As he climbed up the steps, Masih let out a sigh of relief when he saw Hakim. Thank God, there was at least one other city boy, dressed in a suit for the villagers to stare at and make fun of behind his back. Unlike Mother, Bibi Shirin, Khalifa's wife had darkened her eyes and colored her lips with a cherry-red lipstick. Her hair looked curlier and shinier than ever before. Mother, however, had covered her head with a scarf. It was Sori's wedding day, and Mother did not look happy at all.

Masih sat next to Hakim, and Nadia took a seat next to Bibi Shirin. Khalifa shifted into first gear.

Near Sekandar's house, the tomb of the *Shahid*, martyr, was the only grave with a green *togh*, a martyr flag fluttering on top. A frosty gust of wind glided over the river and flapped the fabric. Masih looked at Mother's almost frozen face washed with tears. Emulating her, he raised the palms of his hands cupped toward the sky. He did have an idea as to what a *do'aa*, supplication to God was—a combination of pleadings and whispers of verses from the Holy Quran. Mother looked at the sky, and so did Masih. God was somewhere up there behind the gray curtain of clouds. He recited the *Al-hamd*, and *Qul-howallah* verses, which he knew by heart, and presented his request, "O, almighty God, keep Father safe, free him from the prison, and bring him back home safely. I really miss him." Then, he rubbed his hands over his face, saying, "Amin."

Even though he prayed in total silence, he was certain that God could hear him. Mother, however, murmured her prayers, while shutting her eyes as if she was trying to visualize or remember something. When Masih shut his eyes, all he could see was Father's smiling face emerging from the darkness. Perhaps she too could see him in the midst of all the gloom.

Zaman, his wife, and his son stood a few steps away to allow Masih and Nadia privacy. The gust persisted, determined to snatch Nadia's black scarf off her dark curly hair. But she had already knotted the two ends of her headscarf around her pointed chin, rendering the bully helpless. Prior to her husband's disappearance, Nadia would cover her head with one of her many dazzling, colorful headscarves, designed with flowers, geometric shapes, and patterns. A blend of bright red, blue, yellow, purple, and orange used to enhance the glow of her smiling face.

Soon after Dr. Sharif's disappearance, she fell into the habit of wearing either a gray or a pitch-black scarf. She wrapped and pinned her hair on top of her head first, then draped the covering around it. Even when she went to school to teach her third graders, she kept her headscarf on. This was Nadia's way of announcing to the world that she was mourning the loss of her husband.

Mother's supplication took much longer because she had more to say to God, and she knew by heart much lengthier passages from the Holy Quran—passages like *Aayat-ul-korsi*, and *Soora-e Yaseen*.

Masih turned to Nadia and asked, "Mother, who is this person? Why was he martyred?

"*Bachem*, my son, this grave belongs to a chosen man. He sacrificed his life, his happiness for these mountains, this river, this land," she said, pointing at the fields surrounded by the snow-capped peaks of Hindu Kush. The martyr must have been a brave man. A while ago, Father had told him about the brave men who had lost their lives when they fought against the Brattish colonialists. This martyr must have been a hero just like them.

***

Masih heard the famous country singer, Amani's voice resonating throughout the village from the tower. He sang in perfect harmony with the beat of the *dohl*, the two-ended drum, and the string instruments, *tanboor*, and *rubab* mixed with *harmonium's* supple melody.

Masih had seen parties and gatherings at Qayoum Khan's house before, but he had never seen that many men, women, and children in the compound all at once. The entire village was invited. Prior to taking the stairs, he decided to observe the commotion in the front yard. While children were running around, women had formed their own band of music. In one of the six rooms across the tower, they surrounded the bride and sang along with rhythms of tambourines frolicking in their hands.

"Careful, don't let the rice turn soggy," Qayoum Khan called to Noor in the courtyard. Noor was tending to four outdoor fire pits specifically constructed for parties as such. Flames licked the bottom of giant cooking pots, holding enough rice, beef, and vegetables to feed the entire village.

"No problem," he said with a polite tone. Then, he stepped to the left toward a large grill, on top of which skewers of beef and chicken kabob sizzled. He turned them over one by one to evenly expose them to the smoldering coal underneath.

Usually, at that time of the year, the autumn wind blew dead leaves all about the compound. On that day however, just a few leaves seemed scattered around. That morning, Noor had awakened earlier than usual. He had swept the courtyard and cleaned the *burj*, the room up in the tower as well as every one of the rooms around the compound.

Masih stood a few feet away from the fire pits, the pleasant warmth of which soon turned into unbearable heat. Standing near the fire, Noor kept squinting. Then, he turned and shot a glance at Masih.

"*Salam* Noor," Masih said.

It took him a few seconds to answer without looking up again, "*Alaikum Salam.*"

He wanted to tell Noor that he was sorry that Sori had become someone else's bride. But he kept it to himself. Noor clearly didn't seem in the mood to speak. So, Masih turned around and walked up the stairs. With each step, the sound of music resonating from the tower grew louder.

Tu safar kardi ba salamat—Tu mura kushti ze khejalat
Dega harf-e ashti nabasha—Ba tu qahram taa ba qiyamat
You safely traveled—you killed me with embarrassment
There will be no talk of reconciling—I will be upset with you until the Day of Judgment

The elders listened and nodded with pleasure. Some of the youth clapped while others danced in the middle of the room, flying their hands above their shoulders and stomping their bare feet on Qayoum Khan's *mawri* carpets. Once every few minutes, a breeze blew through the windows and swept the cigarette and hookah-smoke out.

Sekandar kept busy talking to Mulla Salim. Aziz sat among the bearded boys, many of whom Masih had seen in the mosque. Sarwar, sitting next to his father, had a *qaraqol,* sheepskin hat on and like his father, wore an embroidered traditional outfit. For the first time, Masih had seen him clean-shaven and smiling. *Why wouldn't he be smiling? He is getting married to the smartest and most beautiful girl in Deh Darya.*

After dinner, they shut all windows but two as the music kept blasting. The drummer in particular seemed to have fallen in the zone, mercilessly pounding on his instrument. And certainly, Amani did not need a mike to amplify his voice. Although windows remained open, smoke from dozens of lit cigarettes and hookahs began to burn Masih's eyes. He decided to go downstairs and look into the room where the bride sat.

He raised a corner of the curtain that draped on the doorway of the guestroom in which women had gathered around Sori. He could have entered the room excusing a short conversation with Mother. But any of the women could have objected to his presence. After all, he was no longer a child.

149

Three women, sitting in front of Sori on the carpeted floor, played the tambourines and sang the most popular song of the time:

Alaa Gol dana, dana . . .
Oh, flowers thorn petal by petal . . .

Sori was staring at her hands bound in henna, unaware of the raucous atmosphere around her. As a green shawl covered her head, under heavy makeup, she looked a lot older than her age and much more serious than Masih had ever seen her. Several, probably a dozen gold bracelets glittered on her wrists, replacing her usual colorful ones. Sarwar's mother sat on her right, smiling and cheering for the singers. Her long-lasting wish had finally come true. The best girl in the village had become her son's bride.

Mother sat on Sori's left. Masih could not detect any recognizable expression on her face. She seemed lost in her thoughts. The tambourines kept bouncing and thundering on while babies cried and women talked, laughed, sang, and danced. The chaotic scene felt suffocating. Thank God, he didn't have to spend any time in that room.

He let go of the curtain and took a few steps toward the abandoned front yard. A full moon, the chirping of a few crickets, and the chilly wind that ran a shiver down his spine added to the serenity of the night. He could hear the music of Amani and his band, and the women and their tambourines competing in the background. As his eyes adjusted to the dim moonlight, he realized that he wasn't alone. Noor was there too, sitting under the acacia. The autumn wind kept attacking the tree and a handful of leaves that hanged on to its seemingly lifeless branches. Yet, it stood strong, offering the scrawny boy its trunk to lean on. Keeping his head down with his hair hanging over his face, he didn't seem to have noticed Masih standing only a few yards away.

Who could blame him for not joining the dancing crowd up in the tower? It must have been the second worst night of his life, with the first being the night when he lost his mother at a young age.

Tonight, the woman he loved was marrying another man. Sarwar will take her thousands of miles away, and Noor will not even be able to see her anymore. Although Sori's heart belonged to Noor, she belonged to Sarwar, and Noor could do nothing about it.

TWENTY-ONE

Nadia jumped to her feet, breathing heavy. For a moment, she froze. Who could that be, and why such urgency? She wished it were just another bad dream. Judging by the sound of the frantic bangs on the door, she did not expect the person behind the gate to bear any good news. Then, she marched toward the gate, followed by Masih.

Noor stood on the sidewalk. He had pedaled his bike from Deh Darya during the night to get to Kabul. His eyes, deprived of sleep and filled with grief remained fixed to the ground. He looked just as sad as Masih had seen him on the night of Sori's wedding. He placed the palm of his right hand on the wall and leaned against it to catch a breath. Behind him, his bicycle lay on the ground like the carcass of a slain animal.

With her eyes bulging in fear, Nadia asked, "What's wrong Noor?"

He glanced at her face but dropped his eyes to look at his unbuttoned collar soaked in sweat, "*Jang shoda*, there has been war."

"Where?"

"In the village, and . . ."

"And what?" she yelled, "and what Noor! what happened?"

"And," he paused. He knew what to say. He had rehearsed it a thousand times while biking his way up and down the Kamari Pass toward Kabul and zooming through the asphalted streets of the city. He just didn't know *how* to say it. His choking throat didn't help either.

"Aziz and Jawad . . ."

"What about them?" Nadia demanded, feeling her knees already buckle. Masih's heart dropped and his face turned pale.

***

The day before, Baba and Aziz had just finished their morning prayer. The air felt crisp and fresh. It was going to be a perfect day for uprooting and hurling a few slabs of rocks down the mountain. Aziz was ready to take on the day. But, three taps of the iron knocker on the gate changed everything. Sarwar and six of his men, standing behind it, seemed prepared for combat. Many more waited across the river. Kalashnikovs slung over their shoulders and rows of bullets crisscrossed their chests. Two of the men, who stood across the street, brandished grenade launchers on their shoulders. They had returned from Pakistan.

"Welcome back brothers," Aziz said. Then he turned to Sarwar, "how is my sister?"

"She is comfortable in a big house. How is my uncle?" Sarwar asked, referring to Baba.

"He is well," Aziz paused, hoping that Sarwar would show the decency to come inside and pay respect to his father-in-law.

"Get ready for the operation," Sarwar ordered.

"Operation?"

"Yes, what's so surprising about that?"

"All of a sudden?"

"First of all, no one knows about my plans. There are KhAD agents, *mukhbera*, informants everywhere. Plus, Jawad abandoned us, and you don't even show up to patrol anymore. How do you expect me to tell you everything?"

"*If you weren't the bastard that you are, and took care of your own land once in a while, I could have been a lot more involved,*" Aziz said, but not aloud.

152

"Are we targeting their base?" Aziz had been waiting to participate in an armed attack and to inflict some real damage on the enemy. After months of preparing bunkers, and digging tunnels in the mountain, now it was time for real action.

"I can't answer all of your questions right now. We don't have time," Sarwar said with a quick head turn to the right and left, "the enemy has advanced. If we don't stop them now, they will overrun us in a week. We have to act, hit them hard. All I can say is that if we don't go after them, they'll come for us." With that, he tapped firmly on his brother-in-law's shoulder, "Now, go get your weapon."

Aziz sprinted up the stairs to the upper room where Baba sat, drinking sweetened green tea, and chewing on a stiff loaf of bread.

"It's Sarwar. He has planned a major operation today. I must go," his heart pounded with excitement as he stood by the doorway.

Baba gulped a mouthful of tea, "What? Is he back already? Ask him to come in."

"They are in a hurry," concerned, as if he was about to lose a rare opportunity, Aziz waited impatiently for Baba to give him his blessing.

Struggling with his crackling knees, Baba managed to stand without any help from Aziz. Then, he raised his hands and mumbled a verse from the Holy Quran, followed by, "Go, son, fulfill your duty. God be with you."

Aziz stepped inside, kissed the back of Baba's hands, and rubbed them against his eyes. Baba cupped them around his handsome face and planted a loud kiss on his son's temple. Then, Aziz turned and bolted outside, heading for the dove-hut. He unlocked the screen-door. Unlike other times, the pigeons remained still and silent.

He had hidden a Kalashnikov and a few magazines attached to a belt inside a dusty ragged sack in a corner. He fastened the belt around his waist, slung the Kalashnikov on his shoulder, tossed a farewell glance at his birds, and rushed down the stairs. Teary eyed, Baba stood on the rooftop, watching his son wave goodbye before stepping out.

***

Following Nadia's order, the taxi driver, who looked a few years senior to Zaman, pushed on the gas pedal. After zipping through downtown's Maiwand Boulevard, with a sudden slam on the brake, he brought the Soviet-made Volga to a screeching halt. Noor's skull would have crashed into the windshield, had he not held on to the dashboard.

"If I take you to Deh Darya, my car will fall apart," the driver said in response to Nadia's plea for driving straight to the village.

She knew that even if all went right, a normal bus trip would take at least two hours to get to the village.

Scurrying out of the taxi, Nadia, Masih, and Noor searched for Zaman's vehicle at the bus stop, which stood behind the first bus in the queue. Noor marched toward Khalifa. A half-burned cigarette was dangling from his right hand, as he chitchatted with other drivers.

Noor held Khalifa by the left arm and pulled him aside, "Can I talk to you for a second?"

They stepped out of the shade and stood next to a shuttered store. Across the street, Nadia saw the terror in the squinting eyes of Zaman.

Then, Khalifa walked toward his vehicle while Noor ran to cross the street, calling Nadia and Masih, "Let's go."

Zaman pressed on the gas pedal and rocketed out of the city within minutes. Soon after, the tiger sped, bouncing over a plethora of potholes on the dirt road, and over the hill leading to Deh Darya. Khalifa Zaman had never driven as fast throughout his driving years on that route. His only passengers, Nadia, Noor, and Masih clenched onto anything they could to prevent their heads from striking the ceiling. Meanwhile, gazing into the distance, no one spoke.

***

The *mujahedin*, fighters crossed the river and walked through the tall corn bushels. Aziz realized that they were heading for the valley, Darra-e Tangi. Only the river, and the dirt road, running next to it cut through the valley—a strategic location for an ambush, a hit-and-run zone suited for a sniper attack. Six months ago, Commander Daoud and his men had launched a surprise offensive from the same spot that led to the destruction of a Soviet vehicle. The news of his great success circulated in the surrounding villages. To Sarwar's dismay, everyone talked about Daoud's success and admired his heroic accomplishment.

Sarwar informed his men that the assault from that location has to be a quick hit, followed by a speedy run toward bigger boulders upward—not in the direction of the lowlands. A helicopter could drop bombs and fire the deadliest rockets, yet it wouldn't be able to penetrate those mountains. However, if a chopper showed up, hovering above the slopes, no soul would have a chance at survival.

"The boys must have already secured the ambush," said one of the men who walked behind Sarwar.

"That's good. We have to secure this territory," Sarwar said, looking straight ahead.

Secure the territory! What did that mean? Tangi was the natural barrier between Deh Darya and Deh Bala, between Sarwar and Daoud's area of command. Anybody could use the location to launch a quick operation, but no one could lay claim to it. That was the unwritten, unspoken rule understood by all parties. Any attempt at holding or capturing Tangi could lead to full-fledged war. *Was Sarwar ready to take on Daoud?* Aziz had questions, but not an opportunity to raise any of them.

Across the fields, a short climb on the steep rocky slope of the mountain led to a strategic location, ideal for launching a deadly ambush. A combination of boulders and dense vegetation rendered the high ground impenetrable to the naked eye of a passerby below. The environment prevented the enemy from identifying armed-ambushing men prepared to open fire.

"Boys, hold your positions," Sarwar yelled, making sure everyone heard him. He leaned forward and pressed the binoculars against his bushy eyebrows, almost completing a one-eighty-degree surveillance turn. Five feet away, Aziz leaned against a rock and placed his weapon beside it. For the next fifteen minutes, Sarwar kept his eyes on the road that snaked in from Deh Bala. What he should have done was to concentrate on the road leading to the slopes on the opposite direction, where the Soviets camped out. His behavior didn't make sense to Aziz.

Sarwar looked through the binoculars one more time before announcing aloud, "Everyone, the enemy is on its way. Get ready and wait for my command." He seemed nervous, yet focused.

***

Followed by a trail of dust, a vehicle sped along the winding road, heading for Tangi. Aziz peeked over the boulder. He was eager to see a Soviet military convoy riding right into the disaster zone. But, the approaching truck looked like a civilian vehicle. He shouted, "That's not the enemy. What are you doing?"

155

Vexed, Sarwar yelled, "That *is* the enemy, and I am doing what I must."

Maybe Sarwar knew of something that Aziz didn't. Perhaps the Soviets were riding in a civilian vehicle in disguise to deceive the *mujahedin*. Aziz snuck another quick look at the road, hoping to identify the occupants of the vehicle. A passenger sat next to the driver and two men, armed with machineguns, rode in the back. From the distance high above, Aziz could not identify any of the faces in the speeding truck. However, he was able to verify that all four bearded men wore turbans and the traditional Afghan dress.

Aziz stood up, looked to the left and then to his right. On both sides, two men sat behind boulders, holding launchers that propelled grenades. Only one shot would be enough to send the vehicle flying and tumbling off the steep bank into the raging river below.

"Stop," Aziz shouted again, "they are Afghans, our own *mujahedin*, maybe Daoud's men."

Sarwar's men looked at him as if to say *we know*.

"Aziz, if you are scared, if you don't want to fight, then go home. Let us do our job," then he announced to his men, "don't let them get away, wait for my command. Understood?"

They nodded. Except for Aziz, everyone glued the butt of their weapons to their shoulder, with the barrel aiming at the target.

As the truck hummed through the valley, Sarwar let the binoculars dangle around his neck and began to cock his finger around the trigger, while peering through the needle. He was not going to miss that shot.

Aziz pondered on his choices. Pouring in an entire magazine in Sarwar's chest seemed tempting. But if he did so, what would he answer to Sori and Baba?

Then he made a decision. He jumped on his feet, leaped over the rock behind which he had taken position, and frantically waved his hands, "Stop. Stop the car."

Everyone heard his plea, except for the men aboard the vehicle. Thus, it continued to zoom through the death valley. Most of Sarwar's mujahedin dropped their gazes, ashamed of what was about to happen. They held on to their weapons, but no longer remained in position to attack. A few others, however, seemed astonished as well as furious at Aziz's blunt act of disobedience and betrayal.

"Sit down!" roared Sarwar. Aziz raised his machinegun. Sarwar jolted back. But Aziz aimed the weapon at the sky and pulled the trigger. A rat-a-tat echoed off the mountains. The men, squatting in the backside of the vehicle, jumped out and rolled into the river. At first, the driver pushed at the brake. The vehicle swerved and sent a plume of dust and smoke in the sky. Then, as he realized that it was too late to stop or back out, he shifted to first gear and pressed on. Tires spun in place, giving rise to a dense cloud of dust and fume. The truck dashed forward with every bit of horsepower it could muster. It would have had to race faster than a bullet to sprint out of the valley.

"They are *az khod*, of ours. Let them go," Aziz implored.

"If we don't finish them today, they will finish us tomorrow," Sarwar said while keeping his weapon aimed at the moving target. Then, he pulled the trigger. Rat-a-tat . . .

Bullets shattered the windshield and riddled the hood. However, the vehicle kept galloping. Sarwar took a quick breath and then fired again, aiming at the front tire. He missed.

A thick column of smoke rose from under the truck's battered hood. It violently swerved but kept rocketing through the valley.

"Fire!" Sarwar bellowed, looking at the men who sat behind the grenade launchers. The one on the left hesitated, unsure of what he had just heard. But the man on the right did not waste any time. He pointed the loaded weapon at a spot in front of the truck and pulled the trigger. The grenade landed inches away beneath the truck's right front tire. It lifted the vehicle and turned it over. Upside down it glided, making a screeching cry as gravel and metal scrubbed against each other. Then it slipped off the cliff and tumbled into the river.

As the wind howled, the men on the rocky hill remained silent, as if each one had turned into the rocks against which they were leaning. While the cloud of dust still lingered over the road, the vehicle remained out of sight.

"Sarwar, I know it's you," Daoud yelled. He was hiding behind one of the boulders in the riverbed. "Don't fire. Your own man is wounded down here."

"My man wouldn't be riding with you. I don't care about whoever that traitor is. Drop your weapon, and come on out. I don't want to kill you, Daoud. We are all brothers," Sarwar yelled back.

"I would rather surrender to the Soviets. If you had any honor, you would have fought me face to face."

"Okay then, consider your hands soiled with your own blood."

Ignoring his last threat, Daoud then shouted, "Aziz! Are you there? Jawad is wounded. Get him out of here."

***

Aziz dropped his weapon, leaped over the rock, and headed for the river. Pulled by the force of gravity, he lost his balance and tripped. He fell, rolled, and flipped repeatedly. His turban flew off prior to his long downslide on the rigid, rocky slope. Failing to catch hold of the steep surface, he tumbled again, and again, and again until he hit the flat face of the road. Unaware of his bleeding wounds or any of his broken bones, he jumped to his feet, bolted across the road, and dove into the river.

"Jawad! Jawad!" he choked halfway through an uneven cry. With bulging eyes, he tried to locate his brother. The river kept roaring, and the mountains kept staring down at him. He did not hear a reply. What he did hear, though, was a distant rumbling sound of a Soviet helicopter blade.

***

Splashing through the knee-high water, Aziz rushed toward the toppled truck. It lay upside down like a dead turtle. The vehicle was abandoned, and so was Jawad, bleeding on a giant flat slab in the center of the river. His shirt was soaked in blood from shots to the right arm and stomach.

"Jawad!" wild-eyed, Aziz shouted again, scampering to cut through the current. He hoped to hear an answer; but heard not a sound, not even a slight reaction. Was there anyone to help? Sarwar and his men had fled toward the snow-capped peak of the mountain to find a hiding place. If the approaching choppers attacked, returning fire from an altitude that low would have meant suicide.

Lying on the slab, Jawad's left arm crossed over his chest, and the forefingers of his other hand hung loose, barely touching the surface of the rushing water. Like a splashed bucket of red paint, glossy streams of blood extended to the margins of the rock, flowing into the river.

Aziz slipped his right arm under his brothers' shoulder and lifted his head up. "Don't you worry, your Lala is here," he said.

Jawad stared. Color had drained from his eyes.

Aziz looked up. The attack helicopter dipped into the valley, slow and steady. It grew larger and louder by the second, hovering over the rock on which the brothers lay. Its long flat blades spun like a tornado, violently disturbing the flow of the raging river. Then it tilted its nose down, pointing the nozzles of the heavy machineguns, mounted around its torso, at the target.

Aziz nestled his brother' head on his chest and wrapped his arms around him. Planting a kiss on his forehead, he closed his eyes, and recited the *Kalema,* what every Muslim knows by heart, "There is no God but Allah, and Muhammad is His prophet."

***

A rattling thunder bounced off the granite walls of the mountains. Two streams of blood joined and poured into the river.

TWENTY-TWO

Upon arrival in Pakistan, Jawad had concluded that he did not like the city of Peshawar. Walking on the crowded sidewalks was never a pleasure. He couldn't take even five steps without bumping shoulders with another man. The deafening roar of rickshaws, busses, trucks, cars, and motorcycles gave him a headache. Peshawar city lacked Deh Darya's tranquility, the abundance of space, the variety of nature's bright colors, the sparkling of the river, and the aroma of clean air.

For the first two months of his stay at a damp, dark guesthouse, he ate only once a day—mostly because he couldn't afford to eat more often and in part because he didn't feel hungry. Few times that Jawad ate with Daoud's men at his insistence, he felt embarrassed about consuming food for which he did not work. Others had no problem being supported by their leader in return for their loyalty to him. What had Jawad done or what will he do to deserve the care? Nothing.

He had repeatedly refused to accept Daoud's open as well as indirect invitations to join his group, "I need a deputy, and you are the right man for the job."

"That's very kind of you, but for now, I'm going to stay here in Peshawar," he would politely turn down his offer.

In response, Daoud would keep the invitation open, "If you ever change your mind, just let me know."

From the time of his arrival in Peshawar, day and night he thought of returning to the village and resuming his participation in *jihad*. But collaborating with Sarwar would violate every principle that the whole concept of *jihad* was based on. Sarwar's actions contradicted all that was just and all that was moral. Burning down schools, beating up teenage boys, and insulting the elderly had nothing to do with *jihad*.

On the other hand, if he joined Daoud's group, Sarwar will eventually find out. And when he did, he would give Baba, Aziz, and most importantly, Sori a hard time—to say the least. Jawad's membership in the rival group would destroy Baba's reputation in Deh Darya as well as his lifelong friendship with Qayoum Khan. And for the rest of their lives, Aziz and Sori would have to listen to Sarwar's taunts about their brother's dishonorable act of defecting to the enemy.

Upon his arrival, Jawad walked around the city, hoping to find a job that could get him out of that rat-hole called a guesthouse, and afford him a decent meal. At last, two months later, he convinced a supervisor at a construction site in Hayatabad to give him a job. When speaking Pashto, the Pakistani Pashtun placed heavy emphasis on letters D and T and used some Urdu words that Jawad didn't understand. Jawad told him that he had hauled rocks for a living since his teens. His story had impressed the man, and he instantly offered him a job.

His physical strength and determination to move out of the guesthouse and eat a decent meal drove him to toil eleven hours a day, six days a week under the scorching sun. After three weeks of hard work, he had earned enough to afford three meals a day and even save up a few rupees. He decided not to take the risk of hiding his savings in between the folds of his two other sets of clothes, or under his mattress in the room he shared with five other men. Instead, he kept it protected in one of his vest's pockets.

One evening on his way from work to the neighborhood mosque, three police officers armed with handguns and batons, ordered him to stop.

"Why are you making trouble at this hour of the night?" one of them asked.

"I am on my way to the mosque. What kind of trouble have I made?"

"Listen *Kabulaya*, Kabuli man," he said with a patronizing tone, "I ask the questions. This is not Kabul where you can argue with the police."

"I'm not arguing, just going to the mosque."

"Shut up, turn around, and keep your hands up. Let's find out what you are hiding in your pockets."

Although Jawad wanted to throw a punch in response to the insult, he tried to appear calm, following the cop's instruction, "I am not hiding anything."

There were three of them, but it didn't matter. Their combined strength would not match half of his. They were, however, armed and looking for an excuse to put their weapons to use. In addition, he had nothing to hide and had done nothing wrong. *Let them do their search. They will find nothing.*

One of the lanky officers patted his torso, went down to the legs, came back up, and inserted his hands into the side pockets of his vest, scrambling to find something.

"What is this?" he pulled his hand out and held it under Jawad's nose. Holding a brown gooey substance in his palm."

"I don't know," Jawad sounded confused.

"You did when you put it in your pocket, didn't you?"

"I didn't put it in my pocket," he said, not knowing that he was being framed, and the substance on the man's palm was *chars*, hashish.

"Then it must have fallen from the sky," they laughed.

Jawad asked, "What *is* this stuff?"

They laughed again, even louder.

"Nice try. Don't worry, you will find out in the jail," in between chuckles, said the officer holding the illegal substance in his fist.

They searched him again at the police station and ordered him to empty his pockets. Outnumbered, he saw no other choice but to follow their directions. He put his savings, which amounted to one-hundred-forty rupees, on the table. Perhaps during the search, the brushing of the officer's fingertips with the cash that sunk in the bottom of Jawad's pocket, had elicited the thought of inviting him to the station. Then, clutching onto his arm, an officer guided him to a vacant room with a cemented floor, no fan, no window. A wooden cot in a corner awaited his arrival.

Throughout the night, the beam of light intentionally left on, pierced through his eyes. An empty stomach, the uncomfortable cot, sweat crawling down his skin, and the concrete walls appearing to close in on him second by second rendered him sleepless. He thought about those doves locked in the cage. At least, they had a window and a screen door to look through. He made a promise to himself. If he ever returned home, he will let them free for good.

The next afternoon, someone opened the door, peeked in, and interrupted Jawad's staring at the ceiling, "Get up. You are free to go."

Before heading for the giant gate of the high-walled compound, Jawad asked the mustached officer, who spoke with authority to his staff, "May I have my money back?"

"What money? There is no record of money. The only thing that came out of your pocket was hashish. Instead of thanking us for forgiving your crime, you are asking for money? Get the hell out of here before I lock you up again," he yelled, pointing his finger at the exit. Feeling dishonored, humiliated, and angry, Jawad ambled toward the gate, determined not to walk through it ever again.

***

A month later, a lookalike of the three police officers that Jawad had encountered earlier, stepped forward on a sidewalk to "search" him. Jawad immediately stepped back to stay out of his reach. His defiance angered the officer, who raised his baton and swung it decisively, threatening to land it on Jawad's forehead. Jawad backed away again.

Further emboldened, the cop kept charging while still trying to grab hold of his vest. Jawad wasted no time in seizing the pencil-thin wrist of the assailant with a grip used to lifting and pushing rocks and boulders around. Meanwhile, with the other hand, he caught the stick that was about to land and split his skull. A quick twist and jerk brought tears to the officer's eyes, prompting him to let go of the baton. Now, armed with the stick, Jawad intended to land it on the man's right temple. And if he did, he realized that the officer's skull would shatter. So he changed his mind and instead went for his gut. But he missed, and landed the weapon on his ribcage instead. As the cop crouched on his heels, Jawad dropped the stick and ran.

After the incident, fear of arrest haunted him every time he stepped out of his room. Surveying the streets and alleys with wary eyes, Jawad varied the times and routes of his commute to and from work and the mosque. He steered away whenever he saw a cop. As an Afghan refugee, he was a prey to any Pakistani police. What if eventually, he became trapped again? And if the police discovered that he was the one who had mistreated their colleague, he would rot in Peshawar's infamous Central Prison.

Over time, fear of arrest and feelings of nostalgia for his simple life in Deh Darya intensified his desire to return home. But *nang,* shame of abandoning his village and his elderly father bothered him the most. In addition, it was *be-ghairati,* dishonorable to leave his compatriots alone to deal with the Soviets. What would have happened if every man his age evaded *jihad* and escaped to Pakistan? The precious time he should have spent fighting against the Soviets was being wasted playing cat and mouse with the Pakistani police. A few times, Jawad had planned to head back to the village, but the thought of falling into Sarwar's trap had prevented him from implementing his plan.

Leaving Peshawar for his sister's house in Quetta city was not an option either; it simply didn't make sense. Sori's house was Sarwar's house, and not wanting to deal with him was the reason he left Deh Darya in the first place. No, he would rather spend his entire life in the dungeons of Peshawar than to seek refuge from Sarwar.

***

Three weeks passed, until one Friday morning Daoud knocked on his door. He had just returned from Deh Bala the night before, and while at home, he had made a personal visit to Baba's house instead of sending one of his men to inform him that his son had made it safely to Peshawar.

"Aziz is doing fine, but Baba seems to be getting a little weak. He was worried about you," Daoud lied with a straight face.

Tell him not to worry about us. Just focus on your life and work. God willing, peace will eventually come, and everything will be okay. That was the real message that Baba had asked Daoud to convey to his son.

"I am leaving for Deh Bala again next month. You can join me if you want. You'll get to see your father and brother. At the same time, you can spend some time with my boys. If you like hanging out with us, you're welcome to stay," Daoud said, taking yet another shot at recruiting Jawad into his group.

Tempted by his rehearsed speech and tired of wasting his life in a place where he didn't belong, Jawad happily and yet reluctantly agreed to accompany him on his trip back home. He would return only to visit family for a short time. Meanwhile, if Daoud's group happened to get into a skirmish with the Soviets, even better.

**

They treaded their way through rows of mountains that rippled from Shamshad Peak all the way to Deh Bala, only less than an hour walk away from Deh Darya. A few more strides and Jawad would be sleeping in his own bed in the upper room, where a breeze that passes over the river, runs through it day and night. It would only take a few more steps. Yet, he had to delay his arrival one more day.

The next morning, after enjoying a late breakfast at Daoud's compound, they began their journey in a white Toyota pickup truck toward Shah Dara. Accompanied by two bodyguards, Daoud and Jawad were going to negotiate and plan with Shah Dara's area commander to launch a joint offensive on the Soviets that settled near the foothills. Daoud had met the commander in one of the mujahedin offices in Peshawar. Since both belonged to the same organization and operated in the same region, they had agreed to meet for lunch and work out the details of the attack, once returned to Afghanistan.

Jawad accepted Daoud's request to join him at the meeting. Visiting home a day late was the price he could afford to pay for everything his friend had done for him.

The operation itself was well worth the sacrifice. It was exciting to organize an attack that could deliver a serious blow to the Soviets. Moreover, if Jawad had walked into the village in broad daylight, most likely, a villager or two could spot him. That meant the news of his arrival would spread throughout the village before he could finish his first cup of green tea at home. He didn't want to put himself in the humiliating position of explaining to Sarwar the reason for his sudden disappearance and unannounced return.

The safest choice then, seemed to be a secret entry into the village in the dark. Therefore, they planned to stop near Deh Darya on the way back from the meeting. Jawad would quickly dismount and zip through the vinery toward home. No one would notice. He couldn't wait to see the surprised look on Baba and Aziz's faces.

TWENTY-THREE

As Masih stepped out of the bus, he saw a crowd exiting Baba Sekandar's house and walking toward the cemetery. At the front, Baba kept his gaze fixed on the snowcapped peaks of the Hindu Kush. The stolid look on his face betrayed the sorrow burning in his chest and the ache coiling in his heart. Qayoum Khan walked on one and Mulla Salim on his other, twirling prayer beads in their hands. The rest of Deh Darya's men followed them. The crowd mumbled and chanted verses from the Holy Quran.

The younger men competed for a space to shoulder the coffins that the crowd carried side by side.

Masih closed his eyes, hoping that by the time he opened them, Baba, the people following him, and the coffins, everything would somehow disappear. He hoped to be rescued from the nightmare. But when he opened his eyes, he could see and hear even clearer than before. Masih had never seen the sky as blue, the mountains as jagged and high, or heard the river as violent and boisterous. His senses confirmed that the brothers were indeed martyred. Sorrow chocked his throat and tears flooded his eyes.

A soft wind fluttered the green *togh*, flag mounted on the tomb of Deh Darya's first Soviet War martyr. Right next to it, villagers had already dug two other graves. Masih could smell the damp soil piled up next to the holes.

Then, he glanced over at Baba's house. This time, he seriously doubted that he was awake. On the rooftop, next to the dove-house there stood the man that had disappeared from his life long ago.
Every time Masih had entered a shrine, or knelt in a mosque, and every time he had held his hands up to pray, he had asked God to let him see his father again.

Father was standing on the rooftop. He was dressed in the same outfit that he was wearing on the night the intelligence officers had taken him away. Two other men of stronger built stood behind him. Masih couldn't distinguish the contours of their faces, but without a doubt, the inconspicuous fluttering figures were none but those of Father, Aziz, and Jawad.

"Father, *ona!* there!" Masih shouted, pointing toward the empty rooftop of Baba's house. About ten yards away, the crowd stopped and turned around. All bewildered eyes followed the direction of his extended arm. Mother and Khalifa Zaman, who stood behind him, stared at the house and saw nothing, nothing out of ordinary. Sekandar's house, now a disfigured structure on the verge of collapse, sat in the foreground against the distant jagged mountain peaks.

The perplexed expression on everyone's faces implied that no one could see what Masih was witnessing. He didn't bother to explain. Instead, he leaped forward and bolted toward Baba's house. He ran fast, faster than he had ever run after a soccer ball. He tried but couldn't keep his gaze fixed on the rooftop while running, because he had to jump over the broken branches of an uprooted raspberry tree fallen on the ground. Trampling over weltering leaves and red, bloodlike stains that had scattered around, Masih made it to the open gate of Baba's house and rushed inside.

Heaps of dust had settled over walls, broken windows, and the vegetable garden in the front yard. The smell of dust hung in the air.

Daggers of broken glass clung inside the torn window-frames and lay scattered on the ground.

As one helicopter had moved deep into the valley to finish the stranded mujahedin, the other, the one swerving toward Deh Darya had launched a rocket at the village to warn and intimidate its residents. The blow from the explosion had uprooted two of the ancient trees, slamming one on the dirt road and the other against the rocks in the river. Fire, water, and a giant plume of dust had turned the blue sky into a gloomy gray. Upon impact, the rocket had broken the windows and produced multiple fractures on every wall of Baba Sekandar's house.

***

Panting, Masih caught his breath and shouted "Father!" Then, he dashed through the front yard and bolted up the stairs. Stepping on to the rooftop, he circled around and began to search. He scanned through the garden behind Baba's house, looked down into the front yard and beyond the cracked walls of the compound as far as the surrounding foothills. He found no sign of any of the men visible only moments ago. The vacant dove coop was abandoned, the broken lock dangling off its door latch. Was he dreaming, or simply gone mad? The question spun in his mind while circling in vain around the rooftop.

Masih stood next to the doorway of the upper room and glanced around. From the ceiling to the floor, jagged openings had sliced through every wall's bulging belly. Inside, he stepped on the shiny grains and sharp daggers of shattered glass strewn over the pale carpet and flowery mattresses. Neither Father nor Jawad and Aziz were anywhere to be found. He wanted to call for father again, but it would have been absurd.

"Father," he whispered, despair resonating in his voice.

To his surprise, Jezail, the rifle that Baba had inherited from his grandfather, remained hanging off one of the nails, tilted, but still attached to the wall that faced the entrance. A gust flew in, lifting a cloud of dust inside the room. But the rifle remained.

As Masih turned and stepped out, he realized that he was no longer alone. There sat the pigeons, including the three white doves, on the edge of the rooftop, as if waiting for him to appear.

He watched them for a few seconds. Then, he connected his index finger and thumb to form a circle. He placed the circle in between his teeth, just as Jawad and Aziz had taught him, drawing in as much air as he could, and pushing through with all the energy he could gather.

The pigeons flapped their wings and began to circle above the house. Then, they proceeded to ascend and fly away. Within seconds, the flock transformed into a dark circle, diminishing in size, until it disappeared into the heart of the Hindu Kush Mountains.

TWENTY-FOUR

Masih took long and steady strides down the corridor of the packed 747 toward his seat. Holding a black leather jacket in one hand, he had slung a gym bag on his opposite shoulder. All eyes were fixed on him, or that is how he felt. His jet-black hair, brown eyes, dark eyebrows, and a scrawny face, two days overdue for a shave, made him resemble the men who had slammed two airplanes into skyscrapers in New York almost four years ago. At any given moment, it was possible that someone would scream, *Terrorist! There is a terrorist on this plane!* Should that have happened, his trip, the trip which he had dreamed of taking since the day he had stepped on the U.S. soil, would have been over before it even began.

"Ladies and gentlemen, welcome to . . ." The pilot began the announcement prior to taxiing the airplane. Luckily, Masih had made it to his window-seat without any incident. The pilot continued, ". . . the sky is clear, and we expect to reach Frankfurt on time . . ." Masih's heart pounded. It is finally happening—the dream is about to come true. He was going to take another flight from Frankfurt to Dubai and from there on fly to Kabul. Once in Kabul, he knew how to get to Deh Darya.

***

As it did years ago, the scent of burnt wood and dust mixed with the aroma of freshly baked bread danced in the air. Just like the hot summer days of the past, the birds rested silently amidst the mulberry leaves. Masih was leaning against one of the trees, facing the barren land on which Baba's house used to stand. Once host to a colorful garden of vegetables and flowers, it was now littered with nothing but weeds, dry grass, and gravel. The only part of the structure that survived was the well, which still quenched the thirst of the village.

Women and children, holding plastic, clay, and rusty tin containers gathered around it to fetch water. The women engaged in animated small talk while the children played cheerfully. They didn't pay much attention to the stranger's presence across the street. They knew he was a guest of the Khan and Sekandar's families.

***

About seven weeks after Jawad and Aziz's funeral, during an early morning prayer, as soon as Baba's forehead touched the floor of the small living room, the cracked walls gave up, and the house collapsed.

"I begged him to move with me to Pakistan," Sori said from under the shadow of the tree next to the one Masih was leaning against, "but he didn't listen."

Baba had refused to abandon the village or even evacuate the crumbling structure, saying, "My son's blood has been spilled on this soil, and my grandfather gave his life to save it. It will be an insult to their souls if I turn around and run."

Tears flooded Sori's eyes, "Sarwar's men brought the news to me in Quetta. By the time I got back, all I could do was to shed tears on my brothers' graves," Sori said.

"May God grant you great patience for the loss of your father and brothers. I wish I were there for you," Masih said, adding a quote from the Holy Quran, "We belong to God and to Him shall we return."

"May Uncle Doctor's soul rest in peace. He was a great man. Please accept our condolences too."

"Thank you. For me, he has never died. Father is alive in my heart. And you know, after so many years of war, so many heartbreaks and tragedies, I feel blessed to see you two alive *and* together." He smiled watching Sori and Noor sit side by side as husband and wife.

***

As Masih stood up and looked around, he realized that the village had changed, but not much. A few new houses were added while Baba's house had vanished altogether. Beyond this tiny plot of land, the garden with apple, apricot, and almond trees that Baba had planted seemed healthier than ever. Noor and Sori personally attended to its upkeep. The cemetery, filled with dozens of other martyrs' graves stretched all the way to the outer walls of Baba's orchard.

The somber scene reminded him of the cliché describing Afghanistan as 'the graveyard of empires.' He had heard it in almost every Western country he had travelled to as a refugee. *The graveyard of empires . . . or the graveyard of Afghans?* Masih wondered.

A year ago, Noor had replaced the tattered flags with new green, black, red, and white ones on Dr. Sharif, Jawad, Aziz, and Baba's tombs. He had also erected a waist-high metal railing around them. People knew the site as the shrine of Deh Darya. Visitors flocked to the martyr's grave, travelling from distant villages to ask God to forgive their sins, cure their sickness, and help solve their problems. They tied a *band,* a thread, or a piece of fabric to the fence to signify the difficulties they needed to overcome. If their issues were resolved, they would come back, untie the knot, and distribute *nazr,* an offering of food or sweets to the poor.

***

During the street fights of 1993 civil war between rival mujahedin factions, the impact of an incoming rocket had blown Sarwar into pieces. Subsequently, Qayoum Khan accompanied by Noor, had spent two weeks running up and down the streets of Kabul between Kot-e Sangi and Deh Mazang neighborhoods to find his son's remains. But, as the war intensified, they had to retreat to the village without finding Sarwar's mutilated body. Two days later, they departed the village for Pakistan and brought Sori back from

Quetta. Then, five weeks after hearing the news of her son's death, Nafas Gul died of what appeared to be a heart attack.

Months later, on a cold Spring afternoon, as Sori was pouring warm water on her father-in-law's hands for ablution, he told her that he wanted to talk to her about an important issue.

"Listen, my daughter," Qayoum Khan said, clearing his throat and nervously twirling his prayer beads between his fingers, "now that the sun of my life is behind the mountains," he opened with the cliché popular among the elders, "I want to talk to you about Noor."

Why? What about Noor? Her heart raced. The moment she had feared since her return from Quetta had neared. *Qayoum Khan must have made his decision. He will ask Noor to leave.* She couldn't help but feel angry and scared for losing Noor. How could she blame her father-in-law for trying to protect his *namoos*, the honor of his family? No honorable Afghan man would allow a young bachelor to live in the household where his young widowed daughter-in-law lived. Even if the two weren't attracted to each other, people would react with more than just a raise of the eyebrow. They would talk, and the gossip would spread throughout the surrounding villages. Understandably, Qayoum Khan would not allow the honor of his daughter-in-law and of himself be tainted by a stranger's presence in his household. Sori could not oppose his decision, as it would most certainly raise a question in Qayoum Khan's mind regarding her secret affection for his servant.

"I have raised him as my own son. I have already lost one son, and I don't want to lose another. But . . ." he struggled for words, "but I can't allow him to live here anymore, and you know why."

"Yes, I do," she dropped her gaze to hide her teary eyes.

Qayoum Khan studied her for a second or two. Then, with a failed attempt at a grin, he said, "But if I let him stay," the speed at which her heart pounded doubled, "I would have to arrange for your *nekah*, marriage with him, of course with your consent. I want to make sure that before I leave this world, both of you are taken care of."

Like the color of the blooming roses that Noor had planted in the front yard, the hue of Sori's cheeks turned red.

"My daughter, if you agree, I will talk to Noor too."

She had always been quick to answer questions. This time, however, Qayoum Khan waited about a minute. She remained silent. Her face kept glowing as if she was sitting right next to a clay oven. It was her refusal to speak that reminded Qayoum Khan of the expression, '*Silence is an indication of consent.*'

The next day, Qayoum Khan found Noor in the orchard, checking on the blossoming apple trees.

"My son, I want to depart this world knowing that Sori will be taken care of. You are the only man that could keep her happy, the man I trust. It is my wish that you and Sori get married and let life go on in this house."

"You are like a father to me. I accept whatever you decide," Noor managed to mumble through a chocked throat, his voice trembling.

***

On the Friday of the same week, Qayoum Khan invited Mulla Salim and a few other elders of Deh Darya to participate in Sori and Noor's wedding ceremony.

Years later, once again, Sori found herself wearing a green dress, sitting in the same room where, this time, she wedded a man she loved.

***

"So, are you a doctor now?" Sori asked with enthusiasm. Her protruding belly suggested that she would soon become a mother.

"Well, I work with doctors, with an organization called ADA, which stands for Afghan Doctors for Afghanistan, but sorry to disappoint you, I am not a doctor."

"What kind of work do you do for them?"

"I am an architect. My goal is to build health clinics and even hospitals in rural parts of the country. So far, I haven't built anything, but I have some ideas, and I know where to start."

"*Affarin,* bravo. Congrats on your success," Sori's eyes sparkled.

"Hold off on the congratulations until I finish the construction of the health clinic you and Father always talked about."

Noor, who had gained a few pounds and lost some hair, smiled, "Schoolboy, I knew one day you will become an engineer or something."

"It's all Mother's fault. She always made sure I was enrolled in some kind of a school. After I found out about Father's martyrdom,

I wanted was to take revenge. But to keep me alive, she took me to India. In New Delhi, she enrolled me in a school run by some United Nations agency. Then after a year, as soon as we made it to Holland, I found myself in a classroom again.

***

Following Jawad and Aziz's funeral, Nadia had told Masih the truth about his father. Masih too had confessed to Mother about his membership to the Marxist organization. He told her about how Bital and Tofan had forced him to join the group, how much he hated attending their meetings, and how guilty and sorry he felt for keeping it a secret. Masih also told her that now, knowing that the government had martyred his father, he simply couldn't go back to school. He couldn't imagine listening to Bital's revolutionary speeches and taking orders from him. From then on, he was going to be a *mujahed* and seek revenge. That was all he wanted to do.

Nadia realized that she couldn't let her son go to school any longer. One of those days, Masih might start an argument with Bital, or just make a negative comment about the government, and subsequently, never return from school. He had insisted on moving to Deh Darya so he could continue the war that Jawad and Aziz had begun against the Soviets.

But Mother had opposed his ideas, "If Afghans weren't so poor and people were literate, the Soviets wouldn't have occupied our country in the first place," she had reasoned, and announced her final decision, "no, you are not allowed to fight. I have already lost my husband and two brothers in this war. I am not going to lose you too."

Nadia had sold most of her household items as well as the house itself and used the money to buy two tickets from Ariana Airlines for a flight to New Delhi. After spending a year in the Lajpat Nagar neighborhood of the bustling city, the Netherlands granted asylum to the family of two.

***

"Do you have a floor plan, a blueprint or something?" Noor asked.

"Of course, on paper and in my head. I also have some money donated by Afghans in the U.S. All I need is a plot of land."

176

"You already have the land," Sori said, raising her hand toward the plot where Baba's house used to stand.

Masih crossed the road and studied the barren land. He was visualizing a two-story building comprised of five, maybe six rooms—that is if he were able to save and plan carefully.

Finally, he announced, "I think it's perfect for a small health clinic."

"Great, when shall we begin?" Noor asked.

"Well, as soon as we get our building material together and our work force ready."

"I will get you all that for cheap. I have been in the business for a few years. I know some people who can really help us."

Noor explained to Masih that he had continued to work the mountains after Aziz and Jawad's death. He had convinced a few of the boys from Deh Darya to join him. Now that the construction business was booming in Kabul and even in the villages, his small rock-mining operation had grown into a construction company.

"Thanks Noor. Seems you have achieved a lot."

"I am so proud of my hardworking husband," Sori shot an admiring glance at Noor, "but he forgot to tell you that he also rebuilt the school. It was burned down, remember?"

"Of course, I remember. And I remember how sad you were about it."

"I'm glad you do because we need your help with the school too. If you could figure out a way to add a couple of classrooms to the building, it would be great."

"Don't worry. We will make it better. Can you take me there?"

***

Masih sat crisscrossed on a tattered rug in one of the classrooms. The chilly mud-caked floor stung his buttocks. Fifth graders sat on that surface six hours a day, six days a week.

"Seems like this school needs much more than a couple of extra classrooms," he said.

"I know," Sori said, "slowly, we will improve it. Noor's business is picking up. We will definitely have some money to buy at least a few chairs for the kids."

Five years ago, only a week prior to his death, Qayoum Khan had willed all of his property and wealth to Sori and Noor. The couple, however, kept only the compound, a vegetable garden behind it, and an orchard adjacent to the garden. They decided to distribute all of the land except for ten acres, among those loyal farmers who had taken care of it for decades. Those men reminded Sori of Baba, who spent all of his adult life attending to Qayoum Khan's property and business.

***

When Masih entered the living room of Qayoum Khan's house, now owned by Sori and Noor, the rifle, Jezail that hanged on the wall caught his attention.

"Is that the same rifle?"

"Yes, the same one. Baba gave it to me and asked me to pass it on to my children," Sori said.

"May I?"

"Sure, careful though. It's the pride of the family."

Masih reached for the weapon. It didn't feel nearly as heavy as it did twenty years ago. Then, carefully handling it with both hands, he hung the Jezail back on the wall.

"I wish Aunt Nadia and Zeba could have been here," she said.

"Initially, we planned the trip for all three of us together. But because we are expecting a baby, the doctors advised Zeba against a long flight. Although Mother was done teaching her kindergarteners, she couldn't leave Zeba alone. God willing, next summer they will visit and stay with you for a few weeks."

"You will have to bring them and the baby too. I can't wait to see them."

"I will. I'll come back to build more health clinics for other villages."

"That would be great. There is a huge need for health services everywhere. And if we can get our clinic running, maybe I won't have to go all the way to Kabul for our baby's delivery."

***

That night, Sori, Noor, and Masih stayed up late, exchanging stories about their lives during the Marxists' 'revolutionary' period, the Civil War, and the Taliban rule. Sori talked about her long and bitter days that she spent feeling like a prisoner and a slave in Quetta city.

After Sori's wedding to Sarwar, Noor wanted to leave the village, and go as far away as he could. But he couldn't leave Qayoum Khan and his wife alone. After all, they had raised him like their own son. He felt obligated to stay and take care of them through their old age.

***

At the tower, Masih slid up the windows and listened to a gentle wind brushing over the farmland, orchards, gardens, and the river. He stared at the full moon, which sprinkled a fine glittering dust over the rippling ocean of corn stalks, the white mountain-peaks, and the meandering river.

Daoud's land thrived on the other side of the river, most of which was now converted into poppy fields. Even though the Soviets had withdrawn long ago, he was keeping a militia group, called *Arbakai*, under his command.

Masih remembered Baba, Jawad, Aziz, and Qayoum Khan sitting around the room, and sipping green tea while the country musician, Amani sang:

You traveled safely; you killed me with embarrassment . . .

What would Zeba and Mother think of returning to Afghanistan and starting anew? He found himself torn between two worlds. After spending years in exile, travelling from India, to Europe and the U.S., he felt as if he no longer deserved to call himself an Afghan. Maybe he was a citizen of the world. He may have been physically away from the country, but Deh Darya always lived in his heart, thoughts, and dreams. Maybe this trip presented an opportunity to reestablish his roots back in his country. Would his house still be there in Kart-e Parwan? He would have to find out one of these days.

Masih tucked himself under the comforter, closed his eyes, and tried to sleep. As usual, Zeba smiled at him, her perfectly round belly protruding. It would have been nice if she had been there to share these moments with him. Mother would have been delighted to see Sori, her daughter expecting a baby and married to a good man whom she loves.

Masih thought about launching the construction of the health clinic sometime next week, how exciting!

I must sleep. I've much work to do tomorrow. He drifted away.

***

Following the morning prayer in the mosque, Noor introduced Masih to Mulla Salim and his son, Qari Abdulla, "Masih is Martyr

Sharif's son," he said, almost shouting because Salim had lost most of his hearing ability. He explained to him that Masih had returned from America to build a health clinic in the village.

Mulla Salim held Masih's head with trembling hands, and planted a loud damp kiss, a *pachchi*, on his forehead, "every time Dr. Sharif came to this village, he went from household to household to check on people's health. You have inherited his good nature. Your father was the first sacrifice that our village endured. Remember, what you are doing is a *jihad*, struggle unto itself. If we Afghans stand on our own feet, foreign powers will never have the courage to invade us again." Although Salim was smiling, tears overflowed his eyes.

He was no longer serving as the Imam of the mosque. He had relinquished that duty to his son, devoting his remaining time to worship and meditation.

"With the blessing of your prayers we will build the health clinic," Masih said in a humble tone.

"God willing, this Friday I will have Abdulla announce the project, and that it will be every man's *farz*, duty to help you in what you have come here to achieve."

***

Engraved on the slick surface of Dr. Sharif's tombstone, his favorite Hafez verse read:

Hargez namirad anke delash zenda shod ba eshq
Sabt ast bar jarida-e alam dawam-e ma
A heart alive with love will never die
Our immortality is inscribed in the journal of the universe

Masih sat next to Father, looked up toward the sky and began to pray, "Almighty God, please help me with what I have come here to accomplish. Help me build this health clinic. This is the only thing I can do for my country and for my father," then, his gaze shifted to the grave. He visualized his father's kind smile, "Father, I am here to make the dream come true. I lost you too soon. But you have always been alive in my heart."

Then, he recited the *Al-Hamd*, and the *"Ayat-ul Korsi"* that Mother had helped him memorize. Prior to his departure, Nadia had instructed him to recite every Quranic verse he knew by heart at his father's tomb.

***

Khalifa Zaman was about to show up any minute. The day before, he had promised to meet Masih at around 10 A.M.

After breakfast, Masih, Noor and Sori began to walk toward the main road. Passing by the plot where Baba's house used to stand, he paused and conducted another full visual survey of the soon to be a construction site. Then he turned to Noor, "So, once this place is built, who is going to manage it?"

"I know someone who will make a good boss," he smiled, beaming at his wife, "I can say this because I work for her."

Sori smiled back with a twinkle in her eyes.

There they go again! Masih remembered a similar exchange of glances between them many years ago.

"What do you say Sori?" he appreciated the romantic delicacy of the moment. However, he was expecting a concrete answer.

"How can I say no to those pleading eyes?" she said mischievously looking at her husband.

***

A few minutes later, Zaman brought the bus, the same vehicle that he had been driving for some thirty years, to a stop.

"Hop on son," he called from behind the steering wheel. He didn't carry even one passenger. As usual, smoke was twirling off the tip of a half-burned cigarette in Khalifa's hand. His stomach seemed to have shrunken a size or two, no longer getting in the way of the steering wheel. His face looked thin and wrinkled, and the muscles of his once powerful arms and shoulders sagged. But the warmth in his voice and the charm in his smile remained the same.

Sori said, "Masih, I wish you could stay longer."

"I wish I could. There is so much to do in Kabul, and so little time. But don't worry. For the next few months, you will see me around."

The men hugged. Then, Noor placed his hand on Masih's shoulder and said, "If it's okay with you, next Friday we would like to hold a *fateha,* a prayer service to honor your father and other martyrs. It will give the people of Deh Darya a chance to convey their condolences to you."

"Noor, it is very kind of you. I would be grateful. It would also give me a chance to see everyone and convey my condolences to them."

As he climbed into the vehicle, Khalifa said, "We better hurry. Your aunt has cooked a killer *shorba*, beef stew for lunch."

"No problem, I hope your *palang* can make it," he smiled and took a seat behind Khalifa's seat.

"Don't be fooled by her looks. It still runs like a tiger, with a million replaced parts of course. As long as you have a valid I.D. on you, we will get there on time," Zaman grinned.

Masih laughed, "Uncle, I don't need an I.D. when I am with you."

"Let's go. If Hakim gets there before us, he'll finish everything."

"What's he up to nowadays?"

"This year he is graduating from medical school. It was his dream, you know, to be a doctor like your father."

"Congratulations," he paused. Then, as Khalifa shifted into the first gear, Masih continued, "in fact, I need to talk to him. I am working on a project. I hope he could help me."

***

"Khalifa, don't forget to bring him back soon," Sori shouted, standing on the roadside next to Noor.

Khalifa nodded.

The couple smiled and waved goodbye. Masih too grinned and waved back.

Leaving a plume of dust and smoke behind, *Palang* growled and pushed forward.

Made in the USA
San Bernardino, CA
26 October 2018